6/23

D0273055

By Peter Lovesey

Peter Lovesey was born in Middlesex and studied at Hampton Grammar School and Reading University, where he met his wife Jax. He won a competition with his first crime fiction novel, *Wobble to Death*, and has never looked back, with his numerous books winning and being shortlisted for nearly all the prizes in the international crime writing world.

He was Chairman of the Crime Writers' Association and has been presented with Lifetime Achievement awards both in the UK and the US.

For more info, visit Peter's website at www.peter-lovesey.com

Peter
LOVESEY

Wobble
to Death

sphere

SPHERE

First published by Macmillan in 1970
This reissue published by Sphere in 2018

1 3 5 7 9 10 8 6 4 2

A CIP catalogue record for this book
is available from the British Library.

ISBN 978-0-7515-7252-0

Typeset in New Baskerville by M Rules
Printed and bound in Great Britain by
Clays Ltd, St Ives plc

Papers used by Sphere are from well-managed forests
and other responsible sources.

MIX
Paper from
responsible sources
FSC® C104740

Sphere
An imprint of
Little, Brown Book Group
Carmelite House
50 Victoria Embankment
London EC4Y 0DZ

An Hachette UK Company
www.hachette.co.uk

www.littlebrown.co.uk

Author's Note

The characters in this novel are fictitious, but the setting is authentic. Six-day 'Go As You Please Contests' – or 'Wobbles' – were instituted by Sir John Astley in March 1878, and became very popular on both sides of the Atlantic in the eighties. An Englishman, George Littlewood, set the record of 623¾ miles in New York in 1888, in spite of his foot being burned during the race, when his alcohol bath caught fire. In 1966 a physiologist, B. B. Lloyd, writing in *Advancement of Science*, described Littlewood's feat as 'probably about the maximum sustained output of which the human frame is capable'.

I am grateful to the staffs of the British Museum Newspaper Library and the Islington Public Library for their help in research.

P.L.

1

Monday

The 12.05 a.m. trundled out of Highbury and Islington station and along the line. Its rhythmic snorts were replaced by unmechanical sounds. Harsh, stomach-wrenching coughs echoed in the tunnel leading to the platform. Then the clatter of heavily shod boots and shoes. The unexpected influx of midnight passengers massed at the barrier, every one muffled to the eyebrows and topped with a cap or bowler. A ticket collector, scowling under his cheese-cutter, came out to draw back the grille. They filed through, out of the booking-hall and into a dense fog.

Several clustered under a lamp, lighting cigars. They had arrived together and they chatted as old friends. One shouted into the mist for a cab. Minutes passed and none came. Their talk became less spirited, and they gave more attention to the business of getting hansoms. Rather than stand shivering any longer they resigned themselves to groping for half a mile along Upper Street after the others.

They were the Press.

In the covered way leading from Islington Green to the Agricultural Hall, where the fog had penetrated, but less densely, other men of poorer class, bowed by the weight of sacks or battered portmanteaux, slunk along the passage forming a grotesque caravan.

They were the athletes.

Inside the Hall at this first hour on a Monday morning in November 1879 the scene was almost as murky as the streets. The large star chandeliers, fourteen of them with forty-eight burners on each, were alight, but the gas was turned low. The mist around each flame formed a bluish nebula, a will-o'-the-wisp hovering in mid-air.

In these conditions one could not appreciate the vastness of the building, for its opposite end was obscured by the fog. But if a man had walked for a minute towards the Liverpool Road end its glass and iron façade would have appeared through the gloom; the Hall was nearly four hundred feet long. When it was built in the sixties the contractors used over a thousand tons of iron for the framework. No one estimated the weight of the glass in the building, but its arched roof, 76 feet high, and spanning 130 feet, was fully glazed. It gave splendid illumination during daylight. At night, in this November fog, it might not have been there.

The reporters sacrificed none of their time inspecting the arena erected for the week's entertainment. They headed for the bar at the opposite side of the Hall. There – in an atmosphere made denser by tobacco smoke – beer and boisterous conversation revived them and some of the athletes as well. Others, more Spartan in their preparation, found their quarters, where their trainers began massaging them with flesh-brushes. The race was due to start at one, in fifteen minutes, and continue until the following Saturday night.

'Seen some lively shows in this building,' the *Illustrated London News* man announced between cognacs. 'Any of you here in sixty-four when the twelve-foot croc got out of its tank? It stood over there by the Berners Road entrance, swinging its tail vicious enough to snap a man's two legs. Only a month or two before that Patti gave a concert from almost the same spot. Not ten years back we had the bull fights. Remember?'

'Bloody fiasco that was.'

'Oh, I'll grant you that. All I'm saying is every kind of show's been tried here. Remember the royal ball in the sixties, when they did the place up so you'd not know it? Palatial it was.'

'There were them bible-thumping meetings, four years back,' another voice added. 'Ten weeks I had listening to them blooming Yankees, Sankey and Moody. Scarcely a night away from it. My editor had me there on my first job, night after bloody night looking for a story. I know this blooming place all right.'

'But even so,' the *Illustrated London News* man interpolated, 'in fifteen years of reporting exhibitions and spectacles in this deuced Hall, I've seen nothing so infernally barbarous as a six-day race. For cruelty, knuckle-fighting don't compare with it.'

A row of a dozen wood-and-canvas huts lined the end

of the Hall farthest from the main entrance. In one of these nine-foot-square shacks three men were making final preparations. One embrocated his legs with whisky, which he frequently upended and drank. The others, twin brothers, discussed strategy. The dominant twin had appointed himself trainer. He spent these last minutes heaping reassurance on his brother, watched with amusement by the hardened old runner who shared the hut.

'You got to take the first hundred fast. Get well in front, Bill, and we'll ease up later. When we're a hundred in credit, I'll see what shape you're in, mate, and plan the next couple of days according.'

Billy Reid, strong, burly, but an innocent, nodded glumly.

'And don't take account of no one but me, Bill. Them as offer advice do it for no good reason. I've seen some here as crooked as rattlesnakes. We got our plan boy, and we hold to it. You're shivering, mate. Here, I'll give your shoulders a rub with the horsehair gloves.'

Billy submitted to vigorous massage. 'You got my gruel ready for when I need it, Jack?'

'I'll try to take it on the run. Wash it down with egg and port.'

'It'll be ready when you want it, mate. Not till you've earned it, mind. Put your legs up and I'll loosen them a bit.'

The Reids' room-mate tipped the residue of the liniment down his gullet and belched gratifyingly.

'This your first mix, son?'

'Well, I done fifty on the Watford Road last year—'

'He's all right for five hundred easy,' broke in Jack Reid.

4

'Like a bloody bull, this boy is, ain't you? I never seen him tire yet.'

'This your first mix?' repeated the other, unimpressed, ignoring Jack.

Billy nodded.

'What's your training been?'

'The bloody best,' Jack affirmed. 'No butter, sugar or cheese since August. Purging with Cockle's pills. His feet won't blister, neither. We've had them in alum and water regular. And he's run on the roads two hours daily these six weeks.'

'Backed him, have you?'

'Course I have. Billy can't lose.'

'You ever seen a six-day before?'

Jack Reid was impervious to the sarcasm in these questions.

'No need, mate. We know what needs to be done. Billy's got five hundred in him easy. He won't quit.'

The older runner eyed Billy's muscled physique before delivering his verdict.

'If you make two-fifty you'll be on your bloody knees.'

In the Hall the gas was being turned up, a cue for competitors and officials to make their way to the start.

Glasses were emptied at the bar. The Press representatives emerged warmer and more receptive. Through the mist in the direction of the huts came the athletes.

The majority moved more like sacrificial victims than gladiators striding into the arena. Even allowing

5

for pre-race nerves and the numbing cold, they made a bizarre spectacle. Several were clearly overweight for distance running. Others were emaciated and senile by sporting standards. Perhaps eight, including Billy Reid, looked likely to survive the first few hours of the race. With trainers in attendance, applying frantic eleventh-hour massage, they grouped apprehensively in the centre of the arena like penned sheep.

The better lighting revealed the preparations made for this promotion. High wooden stands surrounded two concentric tracks of loam, faced with sifted gravel. The outer circuit was fenced with 3-foot 6-inch wooden palings. There was room in front of the stands for several thousand standing spectators. Hundreds more could watch from the gallery above the stands. Below the grand organ at the Islington Green end there was an arena reserved for the band, who would play during the day and evening. Flags of the Empire hung from many of the girders.

A bowler-hatted official lifted a megaphone to his mouth.

'Attention please, gentlemen! Timekeepers and laptakers to the start, please. Competitors assemble on the tracks.'

'There's your field, then,' one reporter observed. 'Care to wager on the ones that finish the week in coffins?'

'Not many of those poor coves could afford a decent burial,' was the reply. 'I hope they've the sense to quit before they collapse. My Lord! Just look at that one!' A late arrival from the changing-huts clambered at a second attempt over the crowd barrier and joined the

6

shivering group in the centre. He was scarcely five feet high, bearded and with a chalk-like complexion. He blinked through expensive gold-rimmed spectacles at the other competitors and began energetically running on the spot.

His rivals regarded him with the look of bemused indifference that cows give to passing trains.

'If that's a pedestrian I'm Fred Archer,' the massive *Sporting Life* representative declared. 'Looks to me like a plucked chicken left here from the Poultry Show last week.'

Numbers were being pinned to the entrants' jerseys. The Press checked the names of the lesser-known.

'Who's the tich, then? Number twelve, is he? "F. H. Mostyn-Smith." Double-barrel for a half-pint measure, eh?'

'Where's Chadwick, then? If he ain't shown up I'm away to the bar.'

'Chadwick?' repeated one of the Fleet Street's oldest scribes. 'That mean bastard won't put a foot outside his tent until the others are toeing the scratch. You'll see. Probably in there now waxing his moustache. It don't do to let the Regiment down, y'know.'

Two turret-shaped tents stood inside the track perimeter. Their awnings were cone-shaped and edged with perforations, in the style of medieval jousting-tents. These had been reserved for the Galahads of pedestrianism. Over one of the tents there hung, limply, in miniature, the colours of the Third Dragoon Guards. Inside, Erskine Chadwick, champion walker of England, was issuing final instructions to his trainer.

'Champagne with the boiled fowl at dinner, Harvey, and claret tonight. You have the sole for broiling, do you? Now the socks. I shall want a change at noon. Be sure to air the new pair for at least two hours. And I shall want you to have a sponge and vinegar ready in case I require it later, when the walking heats my body. You may put on my boots now. Lace them firmly, but not tightly.'

Harvey sprinkled dusting powder into the porpoise-skins, a pair fashioned for this race by Chadwick's Regimental cord-wainer. Then he attached them expertly to the celebrated feet. His limited knowledge of athletics was more than compensated by his long service as a batman.

'I shall expect Darrell to start at a rush,' Chadwick continued, speaking more to himself than Harvey, 'but this is as I plan. The man knows nothing of tactics. My wind and staying powers are well superior to his, and I shall bide my time.'

'What about them others, sir?'

Chadwick got to his feet, studied the line of his chin in the mirror that Harvey held for him, and pulled aside the tent-flap.

'I shall try to ignore their presence,' he replied. 'Did you ever see such an unwholesome crowd?'

Shuddering, he marched over to the starting-line.

2

'For the benefit of those of you unable to read I shall repeat the rules. You may go as you please for six days and nights, finishing next Saturday evening at half past ten o'clock. Each of you is allowed one attendant, who may hand you refreshments as you pass the area marked on the tracks, but attendants must keep off the path. You are not allowed to wear spiked boots or shoes. Any man who willfully jostles or blunders an opponent will be disqualified. The judges have sole control over the race and their decision is to be final and conclusive. Five hundred pounds and the belt to the winner, the Champion Pedestrian of the World. I won't go through the list of prize money, as you'll know that better than the rules. Are there any questions, then?'

The line of competitors was as animated as mourners beside a grave.

'Very well, then. Bloody good luck to you all. Are you ready? Then go! ... You poor bastards.'

The final aside was for the amusement of the Press. The starters had already lurched into frantic movement, recklessly crashing elbows, fists and boots as they strove for a passage on the narrow track. They moved quickly – quicker than many of them had planned – but gooseflesh dictated tactics. The gas was now at its highest, but dimly lit the vast hall, and made no impression on the near-zero temperature. Press and officials, swathed in long overcoats, formed a compact group in the centre, under a canopy of warm breath and cigar smoke. The stands were empty.

There were two classes of competitor. On the inner one-eighth of a mile track moved the stars, the super-novas Chadwick and Darrell, each a five-hundred miler, while the fourteen less heavenly bodies moved in an outer orbit of one-seventh of a mile. They combated the cold in their own way, most of them with caps, mufflers, gloves and trousers. The rules about dress had set standards of minimum decency – exposure of flesh was limited to the areas above the neck and below the knees, and the fore-arms – which were unlikely to be flouted in November.

The entry had been limited to 'proven pedestrians,' for a large number of vagrants and fortune-seekers had been attracted by the hand-bills and posters.

'Six Days' Pedestrian Contest at the Agricultural Hall, Islington. Sweepstakes of 10 sovs each, for proven pedes-trians; each competitor to make, by running or walking, the best of his way on foot (without assistance) for six days and nights – i.e. to start at 1 o'clock a.m. on Monday, 18 November 1879, and finish at half past 10 o'clock p.m. on the following Saturday. The man accomplishing the great-est distance in the specified time to be the Champion

Pedestrian of the World, and to have entrusted to his keeping a belt, value £100, and receive £500; second £100, third £50; and any competitor covering a distance of 460 miles to receive back his stake with an additional £10. Any competitor (other than the first three men) covering more than 500 miles to have an additional £5 for every three miles over the 500 miles, such an amount not to exceed £40.'

Warmed by the exertions of the opening lap, each entrant soon settled to his formula for earning the £500. Several aped the illustrious Chadwick, striding immaculately, the fairest of walkers. Others ran far ahead, lapping at a suicidal pace. Darrell, Chadwick's challenger on the inner track, trotted steadily, already showing an even, economical action. Timekeepers and lap-takers, harassed by the frequent changes of order, silently regretted agreeing to help.

Erskine Chadwick marched briskly, head high, shoulders straight, arms swinging smartly across a slightly inflated chest, leading leg quite straight, exhibiting the style that had made him champion of England, and the world, for that matter. On track or between turnpikes he had outclassed every challenger in the past decade. Unlike most of the riff-raff who competed professionally, he was a gentleman, a graduate of Balliol, a former Captain in the Guards. He liked it to be known that he made more from his Stock Exchange dealings than his prizes from pedestrianism. As if to demonstrate this he always appeared in university costume, zephyr and knee-length drawers. Others could parade themselves

11

in circus tights: Erskine Chadwick, M.A., had no need of trappings.

His main rival of the week, Charles Darrell, had a more typical pedigree. Sometime ostler, sometime brick-maker, he had discovered his staying powers at thirty and in three years earned and spent a fortune by his former standards. Darrell was a runner, or a shuffler rather, uninterested in the niceties of style. Arguably the finest stayer in England, he had been sent by wealthy backers to Paris and New York, and had not disappointed them. When there was a monkey to be won, as there was now – almost a lifetime's earnings at his old rate of pay – he chased it in his own way. For weeks he had prepared for this race to a punitive schedule of massage, steam-baths and abstinence, prescribed by Sam Monk, the best of all trainers. And there at the trackside was Monk, ready with sponge and bucket.

'Easy now, easy. Step light, boy. Spare the bloody hooves.'

On the outer track some of the opposition were already a lap ahead, but they were the novices. The specialists in ultra-long distance aimed, like Darrell, for an even, silk-smooth progression. O'Flaherty, the Dublin Stag, led them, a flame-haired expatriate good for four hundred miles, so long as he was lubricated, inside and out, with whisky. A yard behind ran the Half-breed, Williams, cruelly scarred by a public-house brawl with a former trainer; and Peter Chalk, the Scythebearer, small, wiry, claiming to be forty but since he fought in the Crimea probably nearer fifty. Far in the rear came the entrant widely suspected of having bribed his way into the event. It was patently evident, after ten minutes, that the puny F. H. Mostyn-Smith was no runner, and not much of a walker either.

In the centre of the Hall, conspicuous among the Press who were questioning him, was the promoter of this entertainment. Short, but vast, with small neat features and expressive hands, Sol Herriott exuded benevolence, prefacing each answer with a gold-capped smile.

'No, gentlemen, I am not an original, I admit. Sir John Astley's promotions here last year gave me the thought of mounting a race. The public like these events. Endurance, persistence, the will to conquer these are the qualities of our time, gentlemen. Man asserts his individuality, his immeasurable ambition. Such feats as Matthew Webb's great swim are man's answer to the challenge of mechanization. My race is another defiant gesture. Who would believe that a man might travel, unaided, close to six hundred miles between two Sundays?'

'They run for prizes as well as the challenge of machines, Mr Herriott.'

Another expansive grin.

'And they shall earn them, my friends, they shall earn them. When you have seen the final hours of a six-day event you would not deny any finisher his prize. Am I not right, gentlemen?'

A well-timed glance in the direction of the tardy Mostyn-Smith, pattering past two laps adrift after half an hour of running, earned Herriott some laughter.

'Is it fair, Mr Herriott, to have two tracks in this way? Surely the men on the inside have less distance to cover.'

There was contempt in the smile this time.

13

'I am sorry that you have not studied the official conditions. The inner track is shorter, but Chadwick and Darrell are required to complete eight circuits in each mile; the rest have seven to run.'

'Why is it necessary to use two paths?'

'Why do we have different classes of railway travel? Why are our public houses divided into different rooms? Why are some of my tickets a guinea and the rest a shilling? You know the answer, gentlemen. The first class is reserved for the best. Captain Chadwick is unbeaten in long-distance walking, and Darrell is the only man fit to appear on a track with him. If any of the other entrants prove their powers this week they may appear on the inner track in my next promotion. I have no prejudices.'

The *Bell's Life* man persisted.

'It appears to me, Mr Herriott, that the gentlemen on the inner path are favoured. Even if the distances are accurately computed the presence of so many competitors must mean that they are frequently forced to take the outside in passing each other. Nor is the sleeping accommodation comparable.'

Eyes turned towards the hovels from which the second-class entrants had earlier emerged, in a discreetly dark corner of the Hall, fifty yards away from the tracks. Herriott walked instead a few paces to Darrell's princely tent and pulled open the flap.

'What you see in here, gentlemen, bedstead, gas jet, food cupboard and toilet necessaries, are provided in the other tent and in each of the huts. If some of the other competitors have to share accommodation, it is a sacrifice that they are pleased to make in order to take part in my promotion. I am not a hotelier, but nor are these pedestrians the class of men who are accustomed to delicate living. Some of them, indeed, may find it a pleasurable experience to have any sort of roof above them.'

Outside the tent another misgiving was voiced.

'Isn't it possible that some of these men may injure themselves permanently, or even die on the track, after such exertions? You could be accused of manslaughter in such a case.'

Herriott had prepared for this question.

'Sir, I will bet you fifty that you die from want of exercise before any one of these fellows dies from taking too much.'

His guffaw at his own wit echoed through the Hall as he flashed his small eyes from man to man.

After three hours of competition the pace of the leaders had slowed markedly, and the board at the trackside showed the leader's distance as 23 miles and 6 laps. He was Billy Reid, and his twin brother urged him on noisily as each time he padded past the place where he sat by the track. The pair were becoming well known in suburban pedestrian circles, but Billy had yet to run more than fifty miles competitively, and the bookmakers still offered generous odds against him in spite of his position.

'He won't stay, Jack. You'll need to rest him soon.' Sam Monk, Darrell's trainer, approached Billy's brother.

'He's overweight, boy. You can't carry extra pounds in this caper.'

'Bill won't falter,' Reid replied. 'He's staked too much

on this. I'm starving him, any rate, and he'll sweat out some pounds as he goes. Eel-broth and ale. That's all he's getting today.'

'Bloody murderer!'

Monk was grinning.

'Me, I'm known as a cruel man, but I wouldn't kill my own flesh and blood. Eel-broth and ale and fifty yards to the hut for a leak. He'll never make it, boy.'

'He might not nail your man in the end, but he's five miles up on Chadwick already. That bastard won't get into his fancy tent tonight if he wants to catch Billy.'

Probably turning over the same thought, with greater delicacy, Chadwick marched past them, upright, superbly controlled, the only hint of exertion two beads of sweat at either extremity of his moustache. He was walking well. He could manage five hundred at this pace, but the form of Darrell was worrying. Already he had passed him more than a dozen times.

As dawn approached a few spectators began to appear in the shilling enclosure. Experience had shown that public interest in these contests grew towards the end of the week, when the efforts were telling on the participants. Sir John Astley's first 'Go As You Please' at Islington in March 1878 raised nearly a thousand pounds on the final night and finished in uproar, with every seat filled, and the winner finishing, in the words of *Bell's Life*, 'as stilty as a cock sparrow suffering from sciatica.' Herriott had studied this promotion minutely, and learned from Astley's errors. He insisted that his race should progress in one direction, anti-clockwise. In the Astley 'mix' competitors

16

were allowed to turn and go in an opposite direction at the completion of any mile, by giving one lap's notice to the scorers. The result was confusion in the scoring, and the spectacle of exhausted men meeting face to face and sometimes colliding. There were criticisms of the event in the medical Press. Herriott had engaged two doctors to examine each competitor beforehand and daily during his race. In spite of the confidence that he professed to the reporters he was taking no chance on a fatal collapse.

During the morning Darrell gained perceptibly on young Reid, who struggled gamely in response to his brother's shouts. At seven, after six hours, his score was chalked on the board as 38 miles 4 laps, Darrell's 37 miles 6 laps, and O'Flaherty, Williams and Chalk were together on 34 miles. A mile behind followed Chadwick, apparently unperturbed. 'Pencillers' moved among the crowd accepting bets, and already Chadwick's position as favourite was threatened in the odds offered on Darrell. Mostyn-Smith had recorded 24 miles and retired to the huts. There the Press cornered him, eager for quotable comments on the agony of the race, but he confounded them by announcing,

'I have enjoyed the first phase of my campaign, gentlemen. I did not expect to be among the leaders so early in the race, so I am not in the least disappointed. I shall now take my herbal restorative and sleep for a half-hour. You may, if you wish, interrogate me again at one-thirty p.m., when I shall have completed phase two.'

With a gracious smile he then walked to the door and opened it for them.

Outside, the Press talked confusedly. Nothing, they were trained to believe, was altogether new, but none of them could recall having met this species of pedestrian. How a mild-mannered man could appear in such company mystified them. Erskine Chadwick was a gentleman-ped it was true, and had taken on the roughnecks for years, but he was a good enough athlete to compete on his own terms. He made a small fortune from walking, anyway. There was not room in the sport for more than one Chadwick. Mostyn-Smith's showing so far did not suggest that he possessed untapped potential as an athlete. Why, then, should this apparently intelligent man deign to appear in a 'Cruelty Show'?

'Likely as not the poor cove leads a sheltered existence,' ventured one of them. 'I think he fancies this is an amateur contest, arranged by the London Athletic Club.'

'Whatever he fancies he should be disillusioned tonight. He's sharing with Feargus O'Flaherty!'

They were still joking and speculating about Francis Mostyn-Smith thirty minutes later when he appeared at the hut door.

'If you please, gentlemen?'

They formed a passage for him and watched in silence as he strutted towards the track.

When Billy Reid was overtaken by Darrell the fact was lost on the majority of spectators because of the disparity in the tracks. But Sam Monk made it his business to seek out Jack Reid, who now sat silent and alone in the stand, hoarse from shouting at his brother.

'There it is, Jack. My man's got his nose in front.

18

Forty-eight miles that time and Billy a furlong down. You pushed him too hard, lad. Had your breakfast or are you on eel-broth too?'

'Can't leave him on his own,' whispered Reid. 'Might walk off. There ain't no rest scheduled before noon.'

Monk was firm.

'I'll speak to him, tell him to give you an hour off. Tiring work, shouting tactics. It's all right for the glory-boys out there. All they've got to do is keep moving. Us poor buggers have all the head-work to do. Wait here, mate.'

Without waiting for agreement he marched over to the strawberry-faced Billy, issued instructions, and rejoined Jack.

'Got to be firm from the start, you know. Mind over mind. They need to know you've got the reins, you understand. Look at Charlie now, plugging away on his own. I don't even need to tell him I'm off for a break. Come on now, lad. There's a place in Liverpool Road that does the tastiest kidney breakfast you ever got your teeth into.'

By one o'clock that afternoon several hundred spectators enlivened the scene, and Darrell held a clear lead. Twelve hours now since the start, he had travelled 67 miles. Reid, on 64½ miles, was about to lose his position to Williams and O'Flaherty, who still ran together. The veteran, Chalk, was resting. He had covered 61 miles. Chadwick still walked resolutely on, but had been forcing his pace to make 60 miles, and the crowd were already barracking him. Never a popular figure, he was ready for this treatment, but could rarely have been so far down in a race, even at this early stage. To more whistles he stepped

19

off the track, and a dressing-gown was wrapped around him by Harvey, before he withdrew into his pavilion for luncheon. Other runners, less provided for, lay in the centre of the arena sipping at bottles while trainers or friends massaged them devotedly. The majority took no break, except to answer nature's call. For this they covered a hundred yards which they got no credit for.

As promised, Mostyn-Smith held his second conference at one-thirty. He addressed the Press in the same schoolmasterly tones:

'Thank you for your interest, gentlemen. As you will have observed I have completed 336 circuits, making 48 miles. I shall now retire for thirty minutes, after taking my customary refreshment. I intend to continue—'

Shouting had broken out at the track, and Mostyn-Smith's statement was never completed. Everyone dashed across the Hall to see what sensation was taking place. A sensation it was, for Erskine Chadwick, champion walker of England, was back on the track and running like a startled stag.

3

There was a pleasant relief that afternoon from the spectacle of exhausted bodies steaming in the chill air. A young woman was escorted through the crowd barrier and across the tracks by Sol Herriott. This was not an easy manoeuvre; her skirt, deep green and velvet with a gathered train, was cut without much emphasis on mobility. In the streets outside, a clinging skirt was not necessarily a handicap. Certain cabbies made a point of halting the traffic behind them to allow a pretty woman to cross. But professional runners in competition had no time for courtesies.

A short wait at the edge of the track, with all eyes turned her way, did not alarm Cora Darrell. She had come, the word circulated, to give support to her husband. She was a black-fringed beauty of delicate features, given to cascades of affected laughter. As Herriott steered her safely to the centre his ponderous small-talk was rewarded out of all proportion, until even he began to doubt its wit.

But an entrance, an impact, was undeniably made. For the next half-hour the straining heroes on the track might have taken a rest for all the attention they received. With confidence born of the knowledge that the stage was hers, Cora moved from timekeepers to lap-scorers, from trainers to backers, knowing most of them already, and ensuring that she was introduced to the rest. Once or twice as her husband shambled past, Cora blew a genteel kiss in his direction. He did not respond, and she returned to her conversation.

Sam Monk was standing alone outside Darrell's tent when Cora eventually moved her attention to him.

'Charles is leading, isn't he, Sam? You're pleased with him now, I expect. He's not suffering, I hope?'

The trainer smirked.

'If he is, then Lord help him by next Saturday, m'lady, for he's not coming off this track except at my orders. No, Charlie's in fine trim. No man in this race is better prepared, I promise you.'

She was smiling.

'That you don't have to tell me, Sam. Six weeks is a long time for a man to abandon his wife. And when you return him to me I suppose he will want another six weeks to recover.'

Monk shook his head.

'Don't be too sure of that, m'lady. If fancyman Chadwick runs himself out, Charlie should have done enough to win by Friday. We panicked Chadwick, you see. Had the blighter up on his toes for the first time in his life when Charlie got five miles clear.'

Cora paused to watch Chadwick as he cantered past, breathing heavily.

'The man looks strong to me. He is running at a faster rate than Charles now. I can't be so confident as you are. Such muscles!'

Monk touched her arm reassuringly.

'Don't worry. We know what we're about, I promise you. I've laid a pony on him this time, and I ain't losing it. Here' – and he moved close to her and spoke confidentially – 'I'll show you our tent, love. Tell your fortune in there too if you've a fancy that way.'

Giggling, she followed Monk to the end of the track where the tents stood, and with a gay wave to her toiling spouse disappeared from view.

Attention returned resignedly to the race. Chadwick's gallop had by now become a humbler trot. But in the last hour he had regained two miles and was still travelling faster than Darrell. On the outer track several of the early pace-setters had retired from the race. Billy Reid was struggling manfully to keep pace with Williams and O'Flaherty. It was difficult for spectators to tell the state of the race. Some competitors had taken rests and others, patently, would need to retire before long. Yet there was a prolonged cheer – the loudest so far – when Mostyn-Smith, as steadily paced as a metronome, finally overtook another competitor, an old professional who promptly tottered off the track and away to get drunk.

Solomon Herriott slumped into a seat in the judges' stand and produced a flask of brandy from his jacket.

This was the first rest he had allowed his feet since before midnight. They could not have ached more if he had been lapping the track himself. But there was encouragement in the day's events. These marathon contests were traditionally slow to attract interest from Press and public, yet the duel between Darrell and Chadwick was already drawing spectators, and the news of Chadwick's dramatic rejection of heel-and-toe would make sensational reading in the sporting Press. He lit a cigar and dreamily followed the movement of the runners – if they could be so described – distorted by the smoke. In a few minutes he replaced the flask in an inner pocket, raised himself, and strolled over to his manager, Jacobson.

'I'm leaving now, Walter. I shall rest at the club for an hour and tonight I'm dining at the London Sporting. Don't send for me unless the building catches fire. If it does, take your time about raising the alarm because we're magnificently insured.'

Quivering with laughter and enjoying Jacobson's resentment, he sauntered towards the exit.

On the outer track the trio known as the Scythebearer, the Half-breed and the Dublin Stag were lapping together, shuffling gently through the dust lying on the hard-packed surface. They wore silk running costumes of the professional type, zephyrs in brilliant colours, drawers and white tights. Williams had a cap pulled over his forehead as an eyeshade. A firm believer in maintaining the body's liquid content, he had brought his training to a triumphant peak in the White Hart at

Pentonville the evening before, and he was now weathering a hangover.

'You start by feeling your worst,' he was telling the others, 'and you can only feel better as time goes on. Tomorrow I'll be in prime shape. You poor coves'll be starting to feel your blisters then. 'Ow are your feet, Feargus?'

'A little warm,' admitted O'Flaherty, 'but I'll have no trouble this time, I promise you. My little roommate can give me a pick-a-back for a mile or two.'

They were overtaking Mostyn-Smith several times each hour. His presence in the race encouraged them immensely. He was fifty yards ahead of them now, a slight, but upright figure entirely in black, save a flash of white calves where shorts failed to cover sock-tops. His action was an eccentric, loose-limbed performance. The knees were permanently bent and the lower legs enjoyed a mobility of their own, independent of the thighs, the style of an expert in egg-and-spoon racing. As the others overtook him, O'Flaherty slapped his shoulders heartily.

'Keep going, mate. Only five bloody days and a bit.'

Mostyn-Smith raised a hand in salute, but they were past before he could respond.

'Give Double-barrel 'is due,' Chalk observed. ''E's outlasted some sharp men already. I think 'e might stick it till tomorrow.'

Williams was laughing.

'Not after a night in O'Flaherty's 'ut! I wouldn't even wish that on bloody Chadwick. 'Ow do you sleep now,

Feargus? Is there still the trouble with the banshees? Johnny Marsh, the old 'Ackney Clipper, shared a tent with Feargus during the Astley's Wobble last March, ain't that true, Irish? When Feargus 'ere saw the banshees 'e jumped up, 'it the canvas and brought the bloody lot down! Johnny Marsh wakes up, sees Feargus there, bolt-eyed and naked as a baby, shoutin' for 'is Maker, and thinks it's Judgement Day. 'Is 'air went white in an hour, and 'e's been seeing doctors ever since. Ain't that so, mate?'

O'Flaherty's answer was to spit liberally on the track and blaspheme.

Even Williams recognized that the Stag would not be baited any more, and he changed the topic.

'What happened to Cora Darrell, then? I never saw 'er leave.'

Chalk nodded his head in the direction of Darrell's tent.

'Went in there with Monk ten minutes back, like she was doing an inspection.'

'Inspection! Inspection of what?' The Half-breed punctuated his wit with a belly-laugh that pained his sore head.

'Cora ain't the girl to stand by a bed with a bloke and talk about training, now is she?'

'Seeing as I ain't been in that position with 'er,' Chalk retorted, 'I wouldn't know.'

Now O'Flaherty recovered his humour.

'Well, you're in the minority there, matey. I thought every ped in London— Hello, that was quick, though. Look, she's out again.'

Mrs Darrell swept into view again and glided across

the arena with copious pretty waves and smiles, including one to her husband. When she crossed the tracks only a deft raising of her velvet train rescued it from Billy Reid's pounding boots as he lumbered past so close that his breath disturbed the curls on the nape of her neck. One final pause at the exit, a smile tossed back to nobody in particular, and Cora relinquished the limelight to the less glamorous entertainers.

Chalk studied Charles Darrell curiously. He continued his steady semi-trot around the inner track, preoccupied with his task. He was still losing yards each lap to Chadwick, who showed no indication of reverting to a walk. Chalk addressed his companions.

'What about 'im, then? Ain't 'e bothered if 'is wife takes up with other parties?'

'Charlie Darrell ain't like you and me, friend,' explained Williams. "E's a real pro – a runner, through and through. When 'e goes into trainin', that's it. No ale, tobacco or women. Six weeks of bloody saintly living. If Cora wants amusin' she knows she can't look to Charlie, not till after 'is race. And 'e don't seem to stand in 'er way if she goes elsewhere. Don't care a tuppenny damn.'

'Now there, my friends, is dedication to the profession!' O'Flaherty declared. 'You have to admire it. Now I don't compare with Darrell as a six-day man, but I fancy that if I didn't have to keep my Moira content while I train I could beat the world.'

'You'd beat Moira and all, mate, when you found out 'ow she'd passed the time,' observed the Half-breed. 'Six blooming weeks of self-control! Can't see Moira 'olding

27

out, can you? No offence, mate, but you ain't trained 'er that way.'

O'Flaherty's temper flared.

'What do you mean?'

'What I mean is,' said Williams, as he hastily sought for palliative words, 'that Cora Darrell ain't so different from any other woman – any I've met, anyhow. But you ain't no Charlie Darrell. If you went on the wagon for six weeks like 'e does, and then Moira showed 'erself in 'ere, like Cora, while you were chasing your tail round this bloody path, you'd murder 'er, and spread the pieces all over the 'all.'

O'Flaherty grabbed at the Half-breed's zephyr.

'Hold your bloody tongue, Williams, or I'll land one on you. No man insults my wife. If I chose to train away from her for a *year*, my Moira would keep faithful to me. If she didn't, I'd belt her from here to Dublin.'

'Just what 'e said, Irish,' Chalk blandly pointed out, 'I ain't a married man, as you know, but I reckon Darrell's got an 'eadpiece on him. True, Cora comes up 'ere and parades like a doxy, but Charlie can watch 'er at it, can't 'e? Now you men leave your women on trust for six days and nights. D'you know where Moira is tonight, Feargus? I ain't seen 'er 'ere.'

The Irishman jerked an elbow sharply into the Scythe-bearer's ribs and ran on, privately coping with imagined infidelities on the part of Moira, who at that moment was at home with the five young O'Flaherty's in Wapping, darning the Dublin Stag's socks.

It was at seven-fifteen in the evening that Francis

28

Mostyn-Smith interrupted his third rest-period to seek out Herriott. After some delay he was referred to the race manager, Jacobson, who explained that the promoter was away from the Hall.

'I am not at all satisfied with the management of this race,' Mostyn-Smith told him, 'and I should like steps to be taken to rectify certain deficiencies as soon as possible. The sleeping accommodation is most insanitary. Fortunately I do not propose retiring tonight, so I shall not have to suffer these conditions, but frankly, sir, the stench in that area of the Hall will become intolerable in a matter of hours.'

'If I can explain, Mr Smith—'

'Mostyn-Smith is my name.'

'Well, sir, you will appreciate that Mr Herriott would want to discuss this with you himself.'

The complainant braced himself to the level of Jacobson's chin.

'If he were here, I should not have raised the matter with you, but since you have been made known to me, and you are the manager of this contest, if not the promoter, I am entitled to some action from you.'

Jacobson was a man for ever doomed to be handed responsibility as things were getting out of hand.

'If I can explain,' he repeated, 'you will know that this Hall was established by the Smithfield Club, and is often used for agricultural shows.'

'I agree that the stench contaminating that end of the Hall emanates from the waste products of animals, if that is what you are implying,' said Mostyn-Smith. 'It is

29

evident that the ground there was not washed or swept before the huts were erected. There appears to be no ground drainage. Hygiene, sir, is a matter of importance to me. I shall leave it with you to ensure that the hut which I share with – er, a Mr O'Flaherty, is scrubbed clean and disinfected daily, commencing this night. If not, I shall be obliged to call the attention of the Press to the insufferable conditions here.'

Jacobson gaped at the retreating figure of Mostyn-Smith, who returned to the track for his next session of walking without waiting for a reply. Why did that bastard Herriott have to go out to dinner tonight? Resignedly, Jacobson began looking for some idle attendant to carry out Mostyn-Smith's request. He knew that if he waited to refer the matter to Herriott it would rebound upon him in any case. He was not a man who resorted often to swearing, but the burden of his resentment and the peculiar aptness of the situation overwhelmed him. He said aloud: 'Bullshit.'

Although the atmosphere in the area of the huts was worsening, conditions on the track had improved during the day. The gas was now on again, and much of the fog had receded. Officials still stamped their feet and complained of the cold, and the runners were still mostly well-covered in layers of clothes. But the presence of two thousand or more shilling spectators injected some warmth of spirit into the occasion. Knots of enthusiasts roared encouragement and abuse at the contestants, occasionally inspiring or goading one to complete a quicker circuit. Betting was heavy, chiefly on the two 'inside' men, and Chadwick was firmly reinstated as favourite. He completed his ninetieth mile shortly after 7 p.m., only twenty minutes behind his rival Darrell. Three-quarters of an hour later O'Flaherty and Williams followed. Chalk and Reid passed the same point shortly before 8.30 p.m., and seven stragglers followed during the next two hours. Mostyn-Smith strolled serenely on, scheduled to reach this landmark at 1 a.m. on the following morning.

Walter Jacobson paced the area behind the stands. Unlike Sol Herriott, he was not a man who believed in being the centre of public attention when he was in charge. Experience of management in several of Herriott's sporting enterprises had taught him that it was prudent to move into the shadows when Herriott was away, for that, inevitably, was when problems and complaints would arise. He justified this shunning of the limelight by telling himself that he was 'making a check.' Why, somewhere on his rounds he might surprise a work-shy member of the Hall staff who could be detailed to clean Mostyn-Smith's hut.

As he neared the side of the Hall which housed the restaurant and offices, Jacobson decided to check that the evening's takings had been locked away. In the board-room where the safe was kept, there was a set of decanters. A glass of madeira would be warming after his tour of the perimeter. He turned into the staff corridor, and stopped. From the kitchens came shouts and screams of panic. Fearful of what he would find, he ran through the almost empty restaurant, flung open the service door and was enveloped in black smoke.

'Shut the bloody door!' someone shrieked. From the ovens flames leapt to the ceiling. Two or three of the kitchen staff were standing in pools of water trying to control the fire with water drawn from the taps.

'The hydrant!' Jacobson shouted. 'In the corridor!' By an unaccustomed stroke of fortune he had remembered that hydrants in various parts of the building were connected with a reservoir containing 5,000 gallons. A hose was played out, and in a minute a jet of water leapt to the source of the fire.

A short while later they stood ankle-deep in a blackened room, surveying the damage, which was worse in appearance than in fact. The cause, Jacobson discovered, was carelessness on the part of an inexperienced girl, using a bowl of fat near a flame. She was unhurt, but shaken.

'How long are you on duty for?' he asked.

'Till six tomorrow, sir.'

'Do you live near by?'

'Very close sir, in Parkfield Street.'

'Get home and rest then, for an hour. We'll take you out of the kitchen tonight. Give you a chance to recover yourself. When you return see me personally. There's a job that you can do in another part of the building.'

'Very good, sir. Thank you, sir.'

Jacobson dutifully admonished the head cook for failing to recognize the danger in allowing the girl to move the fat. Then he left the kitchen staff to restore the room to normality. In the staff wash-room nearby he wrung out his socks and tried to brush the odour of smoke from his clothes and hair. He thought of Herriott dining out in luxury; of Mostyn-Smith's threat; of the stupid face of the cook; of the prospect of a night with his feet damp and numb; and he swore again, repeating the earlier obscenity, slowly, four times.

THE PEDESTRIAN CONTEST AT ISLINGTON

Positions at the end of the First Day

Name	Miles	Laps
CHARLES DARRELL	117	2
CAPT. ERSKINE CHADWICK	116	0
GEORGE WILLIAMS	113	3
FEARGUS O'FLAHERTY	113	3
PETER CHALK	108	2
WILLIAM REID	106	0
DAVID STEVENS	103	5
JAMES GAFFNEY	102	0
MONTAGUE LAWTON	100	1
MATTHEW JENKINS	99	6
WALTER HOLLAND	99	3
GEORGE STOCKWELL	98	0
CHARLES JONES	96	3
FRANCIS MOSTYN-SMITH	90	0

P. Lucas (78 miles) and J. Martindale (61 miles) retired from the race.

34

4

A bell was rung at 1 a.m. to signal the end of the first day's running – or the beginning of the second, depending on how one mentally approached the race. Its none too cheerful clanging in Jacobson's hand interrupted the trance-like atmosphere in the Hall. Several competitors either stepped off the track or looked hopefully around for their attendants. Sam Monk wrapped a horse-blanket around Darrell's shoulders and guided him to his tent nearby. In the last hour Darrell's progress had slowed markedly, and blisters seemed to be the cause. He had stopped two or three times to adjust his boots, and finally flung them away and continued barefoot.

'No matter,' his trainer reassured him. 'I'll wrap a calf's bladder round that foot when you begin again. Like running on velvet, that'll be. Three hours' rest, and you'll be out on track for the next hundred.'

Erskine Chadwick wearily completed another lap before marching across the arena to accept Harvey's ministrations in the second tent. He approached his athletics much as he approached service as a Guards Officer; other ranks should not be permitted to see that their superiors, too, required rest. But in quarters, as it were, with only the discreet Harvey present, he flopped gracelessly across his bed, groaning. Running had been a novel exercise. Now his muscles were registering their protest.

'It can't go on like this,' he groaned, as Harvey pommelled the stiffening limbs. 'Walking, yes. I can give any man alive five miles in a hundred on the open road. But this damned circus ... My lungs must be ruined by now. Cigar smoke, fog, gas fumes, cattle dung. How can a man practise athletics in these conditions? I tell you, Harvey, I doubt whether I shall go on tomorrow.'

'But you must, sir. You've never given up before.'

'Never felt as bad as this,' Chadwick muttered. 'It's not really the legs or the feet, though they ache appallingly. I think it's the effect on the brain of endlessly running in small circles.'

'Darrell can't last long,' Harvey consoled him. 'Fair hobbling he was this last hour. Blisters'll finish him. Surprised me to see that. Monk shouldn't let him run barefoot. Tear his feet to pieces, he will.'

'Pour me some claret, man, and leave me to get my rest. But let me know when Darrell goes back on the track. I must keep up somehow. And turn out the gas.'

Harvey was deeply depressed as he fixed the tent-flap and left Chadwick lying on his bed with mouth gaping, breathing heavily, the claret untouched on his table. Years of service to this peevish ex-soldier had instilled a fierce loyalty in Harvey. He knew very well that for the first time in his life Chadwick was mentally preparing for defeat.

There was now little activity on the tracks. Most of the first day's survivors had been happy to follow the example set by the star performers. The lion-hearted Billy Reid tottered on in the lowered gaslight, remembering his brother's words before he left for a sleep in the hut: 'Keep at it when the others stop, Bill. Every step then is a yard in credit.' Another who persevered was Mostyn-Smith, humming cheerfully to himself to sustain the rhythm of his march. A new team of officials had taken over the watches and lap-scoring.

Sol Herriott had returned to the Hall soon after midnight, listened to Jacobson's account of the fire, and shaken with laughter.

'I arranged it all before I went, Walter. Didn't I warn you about a fire?'

Jacobson mustered a weak smile, secretly hating his fat superior.

Herriott altered his tone.

'You acted splendidly, old man. It could have ruined the whole promotion if a panic spread through the building. Damn it, you still reek of smoke. Get along home for a change of clothes, Walter. I'm quite capable of managing here for an hour or so.' He flicked cigar ash behind him casually. 'No likelihood of another fire. I'll check the tents and huts, though. These addle-brained foot-racers probably hang their clothes over the gas to dry them.'

*

Shortly before one-thirty Sam Monk left Darrell's tent. His movement through the half-light to the Liverpool Road exit was not observed. Outside, a hansom was waiting. He climbed in briskly, sat back in the darkness and relit a cigar that Herriott had given him earlier. The cabby cracked his whip and in seconds Darrell's trainer was being borne at speed away from the Agricultural Hall and northwards through Highbury.

The cab drew up after twenty minutes in a long street of recently built terraced houses in Finsbury Park. Monk settled his fare, made some arrangement with the driver and stepped quickly across the pavement and up the tiled path to the porch of a house. He held a key ready and had let himself in before the cab trundled away.

He stood in a darkened, stone-floored hallway and waited, while his eyes adjusted and identified a pot of ferns to his left and a monstrous hall-stand beside it. He deposited his cap and overcoat, felt blindly for his tie and straightened it, groomed his hair with his palms, which he afterwards brushed on his trousers, and called aloud, 'Which way?'

A woman's voice answered: 'In here.'

Monk found a line of light which broke the regularity of the wainscoting, and fumbled above it for a doorhandle. He let himself into a large drawing-room, lit by gas, but mainly illuminated by a well-banked log fire, which glowed orange and flickered in miniature on a dozen glass ornaments and on the polished surfaces of ornate dark-wood furniture. The ceiling was high, but the movement of the flames glowed there, too. Over the marble mantelpiece, in place of a mirror, was a broad presentation belt, glittering with studs and silver embossments.

Monk stood by the door, reluctant to step from the stained floorboards on to the small island of carpet in the centre. If Monk had been a sensitive man, his hesitation might have had some symbolic significance. For the occupant of the tufted island, smiling from a velvet sofa, was Cora Darrell.

'You are very punctual,' she said. 'Would you like a chair?'

'Thank you. I'd rather sit on the footstool here and warm myself for a while.'

'What was happening when you left?'

'Not very much,' Monk answered. 'He's sleeping till four. Should sleep content, too, for he's in the lead.'

'He is all right, Sam?'

'Oh, pretty good, pretty good. A spot of foot trouble towards the end, but that will pass. If he needs encouragement he only has to look at Chadwick. I never saw a man so beat at the end of one day.'

For some seconds neither spoke. A clock under a glass dome on the mantelshelf chimed the hour. Monk spread his hands to the fire and rubbed them vigorously.

'You say four,' Cora said. 'That isn't long. You must leave by half past three. Have you arranged a cab?'

He stood, warming the backs of his thighs.

'Of course. Are you tired? Did you enjoy your dinner out?'

She smiled towards the fire.

'The meal was excellent, but I could have wished for

different company. One day I shall persuade you to escort me for an evening.'

'I like this arrangement better,' said Monk. 'Let them with the money provide the food and wine. I supply what you don't want from them. Ain't that so?' He had perched himself on an edge of the sofa and was raising her face in his open palms. Cora allowed Monk to kiss her.

'And what,' she murmured, 'have you brought to break my resistance?'

Monk grinned with the confidence of a suitor who has already stated the time available for love's preliminaries.

'As it happens, I did bring this. Where are the glasses?'

From his pocket came a flask of whisky, which Cora may well have seen earlier in her husband's tent, with other rubs and embrocations. She pointed to a cabinet sideboard on which glasses were waiting. He filled them generously, giving no thought to Darrell's deprived limbs.

'My name should be on there,' he said, indicating the champion's belt above the mantelpiece. 'Fifteen years back, or less perhaps, I ran Johnny White, the Gateshead Clipper, ten miles at Bow Running Grounds. Could have beaten him easy after six. He wasn't the same man who thrashed Deerfoot. Out of form, he was, and I was twenty and going full bat. Then they offered me fifty to run to the book. Like a mug I agreed. Johnny won in slow time and kept the belt till Young England thrashed him. I'm glad it was Charlie who finally won it outright, though. I'm out there with him, when he runs, every yard.'

'Except when you take his place here,' said Cora, laughing. 'Take my drink, Sam. I've already drunk enough this evening.'

Monk drained his own glass, and then Cora's.

'There ain't much time,' he said. 'Let's go upstairs.'

She was shaking her head.

'I wouldn't like that, Sam. Why do you think I banked the fire up in here? The bed is cold. This is different, anyway. Charles has never approached me here. Here, Sam. Love me in here.'

Monk was feeling warm for the first time in twenty-five hours and readily acquiesced. He draped himself along the sofa and kissed her resolutely.

Minutes later Cora knelt before the fire while Monk began the tantalizing work of disrobing her. She had slipped off her shoes, but the rest was left to him. His fingers coped haltingly with hooks and eyes and tiny buttons. The dress bodice eventually fell.

'Warm your hands again before you touch my camisole,' she commanded him between giggles, squealing as his hands gripped her shoulders and he buried his face in her neck.

'Bows, Sam. They shouldn't trouble you so much. Here, I'll pull off a stocking while you untie them.'

The next layer presented its own problems.

'Leave the corset, then, and I'll manage my skirt and petticoats,' she offered. 'Turn out the gas.'

When he turned she was stepping from a frothy mountain of petticoats. Monk gathered himself. There remained the corset. The rest would not be difficult.

41

She gasped with relief from constriction as the unlac-
ing progressed. And finally corset, white chemise, lace
drawers, black silk stockings and garters lay scattered.

'If I had the patience and time,' whispered Monk, 'I'd
make you undress me.'

Instead he stripped himself in seconds, and lifted her
gently back to the sofa.

'I think you're right,' he said. 'Much better in a warm
room beside a fire.'

Feargus O'Flaherty grunted, turned on his side and
sniffed again. He felt sure that he had not been sleeping
long. It could not be one of his dreams, he was certain,
for he remembered the race, his aching legs and the hut.
Nothing was going to make him leave the warmth of
that bed; not for three more hours, anyway. But what was
that blasted smell, which had not been there before? He
opened his eyes reluctantly and looked across to the bed
that Mostyn-Smith had been allocated. It was still empty.
That greenhorn would probably walk all night. He'd need
to if he was going to make a hundred miles. Grinning
contentedly, the Irishman closed his eyelids and began
to drift back to unconsciousness.

Suddenly the warmth drained from his veins. His limbs
tensed and he held his breath. In the hut he could distinctly hear the sound of breathing. And Mostyn-Smith's
bed lay undisturbed. O'Flaherty slowly lifted his head
from the pile of clothes which served as a pillow and
looked along the length of the bed towards the door,
which was slightly open. His eyes swivelled to the right

42

and left, but nobody was visible. His head dropped heavily back on the pillow and he listened again.

The breathing was still there, more urgently now, and the smell had returned. But what made O'Flaherty's eyes bolt wide in horror was a second sound; a powerful scratching on the stone floor, the unmistakable movement of something large, heavy and alive, steadily towards his bed. With a yell of fear the Irishman leaped upright on the bed – or almost upright, for in rising he crashed his head on the hut roof, groaned and collapsed. The young girl who had been detailed by Jacobson to scrub the hut screamed, jumped to her feet and bolted for the doorway, crashing over her pail of liquid carbolic as she went. O'Flaherty lay dazed and groaning. When he recovered enough to open his eyes again they focused on a scrubbing-brush lying in a pool of carbolic. He crossed himself, swore violently and bundled the bedclothes over his shivering body and head.

Sam Monk returned to the Hall before four and hurried to the restaurant.

'What did you want?' asked the only other customer, who sat at the end of a long table with an empty cup and saucer in front of him. It was Chadwick's man, Harvey.

'Coffee. Is there anyone inside?'

'Coffee's all you will get. They've had a fire in there. Smell it?'

Monk went through the service door and shortly emerged with a steaming mug. He sat with Harvey.

'Now's the time the cold really finds you,' observed

Harvey, conversationally. Monk was silent, sipping from his mug.

'I can't think why they chose November for this bloom- ing race,' Harvey continued. 'A God-awful month for anything. Some maniac fancied it would draw the public, I suppose. A good chance of racing being fogged off and they have to go somewhere.'

Monk continued to brood, so Harvey tried again:

'Of course, this place is a bad choice, if you want my opinion. A bloody bad choice. So big it is that you might as well be out in the open. Indoor sport, it's called, and we sit here in blinking overcoats trying to keep our blood from freezing.'

Monk was emerging from his reverie. He stud- ied Harvey.

'You're with Chadwick, ain't you?'

Caution flickered across Harvey's eyes.

'Yes.'

'My name's Monk.'

'I know. You're Darrell's trainer.'

'I wanted to talk with you. This lick they set themselves today – it was bloody lunacy. They can't keep at it like this for six days. They'll burn each other off and leave the prize money to the second-raters.'

Harvey evaded Monk's eyes.

'You think so?'

'Look, I'm not new to this game. I've seen mixes before, mate. Your man's as far gone as mine or I wouldn't speak of it. Now I ain't suggesting we fix the result – nothing like that. All I'm saying is that it's bad tactics to throw

44

everything into a six-day too soon. Hold your man steady and I'll tell mine the same. It's the only chance the poor buggers have.'

Harvey pushed his cup aside.

'Sorry, chum. That's not our way. If Darrell's lame and can't keep up, my guv'nor ain't waiting for him. No deal. But I'll give you some advice gratis. If you've backed Darrell heavy, get some rhino on my man, as he's never been more certain of winning. Ah well, time I got him on the track again.'

Elated by his display of loyalty, Harvey stood up, nodded to Monk, and made for the exit. From there he turned to watch the back view of the other trainer as he dispatched his coffee in gulps that visibly scalded his gullet. Before Monk was on his feet Harvey slipped through the door.

Monk roughly tugged the blankets from around Darrell's shoulders.

'Four o'clock, Charlie. Good rest?'

Darrell moaned and lay inert.

'Chadwick will be back on track in no time. Here, drink this. Make you stronger at once.'

He lifted himself on to an elbow, and swallowed the trainer's concoction. It tasted like no drink on earth, but he knew enough about Monk's bracers to value their potency above their flavour.

'Fill it up again. God, I need a livener.'

Monk obliged, and began preparing the calf's bladder covering for Darrell's blistered heel. The runner was already reviving.

45

'Where did you get to while I was sleeping? Get any rest yourself?'

'I lay down a bit, but got no sleep to speak of,' Monk replied candidly. 'Now help me with this sock. Draw it slowly over the foot while I hold this in place.'

In a short time Darrell was dressed in his racing-kit.

'I talked with Harvey, Chadwick's trainer,' continued Monk. 'Tried to get some agreement about the pace, but he'd have none of it. Bastard. My guess is that Chadwick will try to break you in the next twelve hours. He'll push hard for as long as he can, hoping you'll pull up lame if you're stretched.'

'What's your plan, then?'

'No plan, Charlie. Forget Chadwick. Simply find a pace that's comfortable and stick to it. If you fall behind, don't try to raise a gallop. Keep your stride.' Darrell stood up.

'I'm a sight sharper now, Sam. You're a bloody wonder. Let's get started, then.'

He marched out to the starting-line, shouted to the lap-scorers that he was ready to go, and set off on his second long stint.

Erskine Chadwick was on the track a few seconds later, the time that he had taken to groom his hair and moustache. He began at a run, stretching those stiff, lank legs into a vast stride which, coupled with the superior expression on his face, suggested nothing so much as a runaway camel.

5

The tracks now crunched under a dozen marching pairs of feet. Billy Reid, three hours in credit, looked ready to collapse at any moment. From time to time his eyes turned forlornly towards the hut where his brother continued to sleep.

'Didn't like to disturb him, young'un,' had said the old pedestrian who shared the hut. 'I'd go over there and wake him if I was you. I never saw a man sleepin' more peaceful. I feel a lot better meself. Uncommon comfy, them pallets.'

Feargus O'Flaherty had other comments to make about the sleeping arrangements as he toured the track with Williams and Chalk. By comparison with his newest experience, his brushes with banshees paled into insignificance.

'And there, as I live and breathe, was the spectre of death come to claim me for Purgatory. The smell it brought with it was all around me, stifling me. Holy Mother of God, how I prayed! And when I opened my eyes there was Death herself, in the form of a woman, stealing up on me.'

'Was that when you 'it the roof, Feargus?'

'It was. I think that was how I saved my soul. I jumped up like an avenging angel, with a great shout of defiance, and she fled.'

'Did you chase after 'er?'

'I did not.'

'Was she a shapely woman?' Williams inquired. 'I think I might surrender my 'oly soul when she visits me.'

'God forgive you, Williams!' O'Flaherty snarled at the Half-breed. 'The man who jokes of death risks his own salvation.'

Duly chastened, Williams altered his approach:

'What did your little room-mate do while this was going on?'

'Double-barrel? I saw nothing of him.'

''Iding under 'is bloody bed, I reckon.'

'Not at all. He didn't come in to the hut for rest or sleep. So far as I can tell he was out here blistering his little feet all the while.'

The three pedestrians regarded Mostyn-Smith, whose steady march continued, with some interest. Unlike Reid, the other invader of the small hours, he showed little sign of fatigue. The stride was as easy and precise as it had been hours before. While others were sleeping he had lapped the track twenty-eight times.

On the inner circuit, unexpected things were happening. Charles Darrell was a revitalized force, cantering through his laps at a faster rate than anyone else in the race. His blistered foot might not have existed. Even Sam Monk, the advocate of uninhibited running, stood with a towel waving Darrell down, appealing to him to case the pace. But with a sweep of his hand the runner blazoned defiance. It was not clear whether his exuberant display was calculated to upset Chadwick's poise, but this it undoubtedly did. Whatever form he assumed Darrell's running would take, Chadwick had not expected to surrender the initiative. His decision of the previous day to break into a run had proved a useful tactic. It gave him psychological mastery. And the sight of Darrell hobbling to his tent that night convinced Chadwick that he could dictate events in future. Darrell would be content to leave the thinking, the planning, the pace-making to him; the poor fellow was committed by his weakened state to a strategy of strawclutching.

Now this cripple of three hours ago was completing his second mile in less than twelve minutes. Chadwick, by contrast, was having to force his taut muscles to work. It was hard enough walking; raising a run was unthinkable. Twice Darrell had lapped him, and now he could hear the boots bearing down on him again. This time, as though to emphasize his new role, Darrell spoke as he moved out to overtake.

'Care to run a few laps with me? Easier that way.'

'Not at present,' Chadwick answered, between gasps.

The infernal man was chopping his stride, talking over his shoulder.

'We might make six hundred by Saturday if we share the pace,' continued Darrell. 'Settle the race in the final stages, but both beat the record.'

Chadwick shook his head, but said nothing, and

Darrell, after shrugging his shoulders and opening his arms expansively, cruised on ahead.

The runners on the outer track were following these developments with interest. Williams spoke first.

'What's this? Charlie Darrell's bloody swan-song, I reckon.'

'What d'you mean?'

'Obvious. He's finished. Tryin' to run Chadwick into the ground before 'e stops.'

'No, no,' said Chalk, from long experience, 'Charlie ain't the man to try that. Besides, 'e don't look done in to me. 'E's 'ad one of Monk's bracers. That's what's happened to him. Two hours from now 'e'll be creeping round like the rest of us. Mark my words.'

O'Flaherty was sceptical.

'It's bloody early in the race to be touching that stuff. I've got a pick-me-up for myself, but I shan't let it pass my lips before Thursday.'

Williams rarely let an opportunity pass.

'Sure you didn't take it as a night-cap, Feargus, before you saw the spook?'

The Irishman lashed out with his arm, but Williams had once earned his living as a pugilist, and ducked neatly. In the boardroom, Herriott and Jacobson were reviewing the first day's takings, which amounted to a little over £260.

'It could be a deal worse, Walter. With the £170 we took in entries we've already covered the hire of the Hall. Monday and Tuesday are never good days in these affairs. Astley reckons to double his receipts on the third and fourth days, and then double them again for the last two.'

50

'There's still two and a half thousand in expenses to cover,' Jacobson reminded him. 'If Darrell doesn't blow up we ought to get good reports in the Press. But the moonstruck idiot is on the track now, spurting like a harrier. He'll never keep going, Sol. He wasn't a sound investment.'

Herriott exhaled noisily.

'One moment, Walter. You're the manager of this race, and you are responsible to me for seeing that it proceeds successfully. I picked out two of the best men in England, on good advice – the dregs and lees don't concern us – and I've staked a fortune on this promotion. You' – and he laid a fat finger on Jacobson's sleeve – 'will see that Darrell doesn't drop out. He runs till Saturday, or walks, or crawls. Understand me?'

'Yes, yes,' answered Jacobson, 'but you understand this, Sol. I agree I'm responsible for all the arrangements. I've appointed teams of judges and scorers who are working well in difficult conditions. I've spent weeks over preparations – printing, advertising, hiring officials, contractors for the stand, gate-keepers, cornmissionaires, police—'

'All right, Walter. You've done well up to now—'

'And there have been belts and medals to prepare, and all the entries to sift. That was my work, and it's done, even if I knew nothing of pedestrianism before last June. What's been your contribution, Sol?'

'Three thousand pounds of my money among other things.'

Months of stifled resentment were inflaming Jacobson now.

51

'Well, I can tell you what those other things are. Press interviews and escorting lady visitors – and one other duty that you insisted on. That was the right to choose the main contestants. And you, Sol, *you* chose Darrell.'

Herriott was shaking, partly from shock, partly anger.

'Damn it, Jacobson. I'm not a blasted clairvoyant.'

'I take your point. But nor am I a scapegoat for your mistaken judgements. I've said enough. We've never had a wry word in all the years we've known each other.'

Herriott stood to pour sherry. His hands still trembled.

'You are right. I spoke out of place and I apologize. I think we have both been on duty here too long.'

It crossed Jacobson's mind that Herriott had spent all of the previous evening out of the building, but he said no more.

'I shall hold myself responsible if anything goes wrong with Darrell – or Chadwick, for that matter.' Herriott continued. 'But you, if I may say so, are on better terms with the training fraternity than I am. I should appreciate it, Walter, if you would have a word with Darrell's man – Monk, I think he's called – and find out what game he's at.'

'I'll do what I can.'

Herriott handed a glass of sherry to his manager.

'Things should go better today. The band report at ten. I'm told they're more noted for their vigour than the melody they produce, but they may help us to believe we're feeling warmer.'

'I hope they inject some life into the runners on the outer path,' added Jacobson. 'No one expects a broken down old cabber to go like a racehorse, but some of them look ready for the knacker.'

At 5.30 a.m. Francis Mostyn-Smith returned to the track after a cat-nap of thirty minutes. He resumed his walk a few yards in front of O'Flaherty's group, and the Irishman, as usual, slapped the little man's shoulder.

'That wouldn't have been you sneaking back from the huts, now would it? I thought we were a man short on this track. You can't sleep all day, mate.'

Mostyn-Smith opened his mouth but they were already too far ahead to hear his reply. So he waited until they approached him to overtake again, but this time side-stepped smartly to his right so that they could pass inside, without the back-slapping. And as they came level, he addressed them.

'You noticed the refreshing smell of carbolic in our hut, I hope, O'Flaherty. I managed to arrange with the management for our floor to be scrubbed each evening. It gives us a great advantage.'

'You what?' The Irishman had pulled up and rounded on Mostyn-Smith.

'Carbolic, O'Flaherty. For hygiene, you know. The place reeked of animals. I don't think you'll be disturbed. I haven't seen the cleaning-woman go in myself, but the hut smells distinctly sweeter.'

'Carbolic? Cleaning-woman?' repeated O'Flaherty. His face darkened as realization dawned on him. 'Oh Father! Keep me from committing a mortal sin!'

He wielded a fist before Mostyn-Smith's startled face,

but words and action failed him. He dropped his hands limply. Utterly deflated, he trudged off after the others, praying that they had not heard the conversation.

Walter Jacobson did not immediately search for Monk. The spirit he had shown in the boardroom had shaken Herriott. He was determined not to surrender any of the new respect he had won. So he resisted the impulses that urged him to carry out orders at once. And when he eventually found Monk, towards six o'clock, the circumstances had altered. Charles Darrell's spasm of energy had plainly subsided. He now moved along the track at a sedate plod, and the limp was back. Chadwick, however, had run off his stiffness and settled to a comfortable jog-trot, energetic enough to make inroads on his rival's lead.

Monk was in the restaurant. 'Emergency breakfasts' were being served there.

'Chadwick needs to make up a mile or two after your lad's fine start,' Jacobson tactfully began, as he seated himself next to the trainer. 'I think he surprised us all, going off at such a gallop.'

Monk shook his head.

'Too fast. It wasn't like Charlie. He knows you can't play about with pace. He knows that as well as anyone. What's he doing now? Beginning to suffer, I shouldn't wonder.'

He seemed complacent. Evidently Darrell deserved to suffer a little, in his trainer's opinion.

'Well,' answered Jacobson, 'his lapping looks a sight slower than it was. Do you mean that he wasn't under instructions to warm up the pace?'

'I never give instructions unless I see a man's liable to

54

break down. If Charlie ain't learned by now that you don't bolt like a goose at Christmas on the second morning of a six-day wobble, then he deserves a few hours' struggling. I got no sympathy, Mr Jacobson.'

'You're not worried about blistering? How are his feet?'

Monk nonchalantly buttered a piece of toast.

'Seen 'em worse – a lot worse. He won't give up on that account.'

'I sincerely hope he won't give up on any account. There's a deal of public interest in this duel with Chadwick. It would be disastrous to our promotion if the race didn't come to a finish.'

'Then you'd better see Chadwick's trainer, Mr Jacobson. We ain't the party that'll seize up, if any does. Charlie's record is clean.'

'Quite so,' agreed Jacobson, who still held private reservations about Darrell's staying powers. 'But, like you, I like to see a man run to his best form.'

A voice unexpectedly hailed Monk from the restaurant door.

'You're wanted on track, mate. Your feller's down with cramp!'

'I bloody knew it,' the trainer told Jacobson. 'He was asking for this, running himself into a lather. D'you know how long we spent on his breathings? Six weeks! He was better prepared than any in this race.'

Grumbling profusely, Monk made for the door and marched out past the stands to the competitors' entrance. At the side of the inner track a cluster of officials and a constable had gathered around Darrell. He lay on his side

55

with knees bent, arms tensed and moaning. His face was ghastly pale. Monk knelt at his side and began manipulating his legs.

'That's the second to go inside an hour,' cheerfully commented one of the onlookers. 'That boy Reid fell like a stone – and his brother couldn't be found, neither. By the looks of him he won't see the track for a couple of hours.'

Darrell allowed Monk to work at his aching legs. The pain was easing. Chadwick jogged by, regarding these operations with interest.

Darrell spoke. 'It was soft to go off like that, I own it. Just get me back on the path.'

'How are your feet?' Monk asked.

'No trouble really. Pins and needles. Part of the cramp, I suppose.'

'Try to stand up.'

Applause broke out in the enclosure as Darrell was seen to be vertical again. A crowd of several hundred had paid their shillings, many before commencing the day's work.

'Now put your weight on the leg. Move around. Are you game to go on? I wouldn't come off yet, or the cramp might take a hold. I'll bring a jacket. Must keep your blood warm.'

Darrell freed himself from the hands supporting him, and stepped on to the track. A little unsteadily he forced himself to trot away. There was cheering from the stands.

Monk slipped into the tent and brought out a Norfolk jacket. He caught up with Darrell and wrapped it around him.

'Just keep on the move, Charlie, and you'll run yourself back on form.'

The runner worked the jacket on and seemed to quicken his pace as he rounded the bend at the Liverpool Road end.

Sol Herriott, who was holding a Press conference at one end of the arena, was visibly affected by Darrell's breakdown.

'Shall we adjourn for a few moments, gentlemen, to watch this dramatic development?'

They clustered on one of the bends, a wall of dark over-coats turreted with bowler hats, behind which Darrell was lost to view for seconds as he hobbled past. Monk walked anxiously at his side, encouraging him from inside the ropes. Then the reporters rearranged themselves around Herriott. Questions bombarded him.

'What happens if he throws in his hand?'

'Where's your doctors, Mr Herriott?'

'Will you call the race off if he pulls out?'

'What's happened to young Reid?'

The promoter held up a hand and fixed his mouth and eyebrows in the grimace of a long-suffering schoolmaster. The questions subsided. Herriott, with deliberate slowness, lit a cigar, and resumed his conference.

'Cramp is nothing unusual in a six-day race, gentlemen. Shall we keep our perspective? If there *is* any question of this man retiring from the race I have no doubt that he'll try the remedy of a few hours' sleep before giving up. And I may remind you that Mr Darrell is a professional sportsman of uncommon long experience. There are stratagems in this business of pedestrianism, gentlemen. Need I say more?'

'You're telling us Darrell's a good actor, Mr Herriott?'

'Merely suggesting a possibility, Mr Martin. You *are* from the *Sporting and Dramatic*, aren't you? Your opinion is doubtless more valuable than mine.' He simpered at the skill of his repartee.

The questions lasted another five minutes. Herriott's thesis (that the promotion was so impeccably staged that it could not fail to produce record performances and a momentous finish) took some knocks, but he defended it stoutly. The pity was that when he was beginning to convince some of his listeners a series of screams rang echoing across the Hall and the conference dispersed in seconds.

A woman was in a state of hysteria in the shilling enclosure. Officials sprinted across the tracks, the newsmen converged there and the shrieking creature was subdued. What had escaped most of the Press was the reason for her outburst. On the inner track Darrell had collapsed again. He lay full length on the track, his face contorted with pain, turned towards the section of the crowd where the woman had been watching. The attention switched to him. Monk ran on to the track and began working at the contracted leg-muscles. A blanket was thrown over Darrell's shoulders. After some seconds of silence the crowd began shouting that he should be taken off, and whistles of approval greeted two stretcher-bearers, who moved the runner, still gasping with pain, to his tent.

A doctor, summoned by Herriott, joined Monk inside

the tent, where Darrell lay on the bed, breathing more regularly and with some relaxation.

'A devil of a cramp,' the trainer diagnosed as he continued to massage the legs.

'Keep the man warm, then, and massage upwards, with the course of circulation. We must get those boots off.'

In a matter of minutes Darrell was free of pain, but the experience had left him considerably weaker. His pulse-rate and heartbeat were taken.

'This man is not to run again today,' the doctor stated, perhaps without realizing its full implications.

Darrell spoke for the first time.

'You can't – I must. You can't stop me.'

His shoulders were pressed back on to the bed.

'Take a sleep, my man. You are in no state to think of continuing. When you've rested you'll be twice the runner.'

With a nod to Monk, the doctor withdrew to report to Herriott.

'The man obviously has a saline deficiency, and he is now totally exhausted. There is no question of his running for another twelve hours.'

'Twelve? You can't mean this. He's one of the principals. These men recover quickly—'

'Twelve hours, sir, or I won't answer for the man's health. The pulse is racing dangerously.'

Herriott sought for words to influence the doctor. Twelve hours meant the ruin of his promotion. All the publicity, all the interest, had focused on the Darrell-Chadwick duel.

'Perhaps ... another opinion. Your colleague, when he comes in, may see the possibility of a faster recovery?'

'That is for him to decide, Mr Herriott. You have my opinion. I am sorry—'

The conversation was severed by a groan of appalling desperation from Darrell's tent. For a shocked instant, both men stood immobile. Then they ran to the tent.

Charles Darrell lay pinned to the mattress by Monk's straining arms. Beneath the blankets his lower body jerked woodenly in convulsions. Pain had transformed his face. His mouth gaped, struggling to shout again, but instead repeatedly gasped for breath.

The doctor pulled Monk from the restraining position which he had instinctively taken up, and allowed Darrell to roll on to his side, where he at last gave vent to agonized moaning. The spasms lessened in number and intensity as the seconds passed.

'Stretcher! We must move him out at once,' the doctor shouted. 'I need a room for him, away from this row.'

Herriott, to his credit, was equal to the urgency of the situation. While the stretcher-bearers were recalled to the tent, he ordered other attendants to erect a spare bed in the boardroom. In minutes, Darrell, still conscious, but moaning with an involuntary rhythm, was carried out of the tent and across the tracks.

As the party moved towards the corridor which led to the offices, a figure in black running costume followed and caught up with the doctor.

'You will excuse me. My name is Mostyn-Smith. Possibly I can assist. I have a degree in medicine.'

The doctor received this information as calmly as though Mostyn-Smith were dressed in frock-coat and spats.

'My thanks, Doctor. I shall be much in your debt if you will give an opinion.'

Darrell was borne into the boardroom where the bed was almost ready.

'And now, Mr Herriott, and you, sir,' the doctor said addressing Monk, 'if you will leave us with the patient? Please do not go far away, as we may need urgent medical supplies.'

When the door had closed, Herriott turned to face a dozen reporters, eager for statements. He recovered a little of his poise.

'Mr Darrell has been removed from the area of the tracks in order that he may rest, gentlemen. As you saw for yourselves, he was suffering from severe cramp – a sign of overtiredness. Please do him the kindness now of leaving him to rest. A doctor is with him as an extra precaution, and if there is any comment on his condition I shall recall you.'

For almost an hour, interrupted only when Mostyn-Smith came out briefly to ask for warm, strong tea for the patient, Herriott paced the corridor, trying to devise ways of salvaging something from this setback. The Press, he knew, would not be stalled for long. If Darrell were forced to withdraw from the race, and the newspapers published the information, the attendance for the second part of the week would plummet. Nobody wanted to see an exhibition by Chadwick, famous as he was; and the rest of the field could run for a year without attracting anyone to the Hall.

At length the door of the bedroom opened, and Mostyn-Smith, saying nothing, indicated with his eyes that they were ready for Herriott to enter. He understood the silence a moment later. He stood in the doorway and looked at the bed on the opposite side, where the lifeless body of Charles Darrell lay, covered by a blanket.

6

By noon the runners were watched by a crowd of nearly a thousand. Boisterous and frequently insulting shouts echoed around the nine pedestrians who were circling the tracks at that stage. They were mostly too bored or weary to react. The arrival of the band, two hours before, had encouraged some horseplay from the Half-breed, who attempted to waltz with O'Flaherty against his will. But now the eleven green-jacketed 'snake charmers' were repeating their medley of popular airs for the fourth time, and their performance was becoming as ritualized as the movement of the runners. Interest was revived, though, by Mostyn-Smith's reappearance in the race, seconds after midday. With a wave to the lap-scorers he crossed the scratch-line and immediately resumed his characteristic four-mile-an-hour gait. Chalk, the Scythebearer, was the first to draw level with him, cutting his stride to keep pace.

'You got called to Charlie Darrell, then.'

Mostyn-Smith had expected to be interrogated, and decided to provide the required information at once.

'Yes. I am qualified in medicine. I did what I could to help. He was too far gone, though. Mr Darrell died about an hour ago.'

'Died?'

'Yes.'

'You mean 'e ran 'imself to death?'

'I did not say that. It is too early to say for certain what was the cause of death. The race-doctors have decided to hold a post-mortem examination. I shall be exceedingly surprised if overtaxing of the system proves to be the only cause.'

Williams, O'Flaherty and the veteran who shared Reid's hut slowed to Mostyn-Smith's pace and fell in behind. Chalk told them the essential facts.

'And this is premature, of course,' added Mostyn-Smith, 'but I think it right as a doctor to warn you all – and I shall speak to the other contestants – that Mr Darrell's last hours bore several of the symptoms of tetanus – a very vicious disease.'

'Tetanus!' Williams repeated. 'That's the ostler's disease, ain't it?'

'It has certainly been established that there is a tendency for workers in stables and farmyards to contract tetanus.'

'But Darrell ain't been near a farm. 'E took his breathings at 'Ackney Wick. Monk told me that.'

Mostyn-Smith was patient.

'That may be so. However, gentlemen, if one needed to look for a building in London where tetanus might be contracted—'

He spread his hands, gazed upwards to the roof and looked resignedly at each troubled face.

'You mean – this bloody 'ole! You're right. The biggest stinking cow-shed in the country,' Williams thundered.

'But before you vacate the Hall, gentlemen, I think it unlikely that any of us will become infected. I have arranged for the area of the huts, which is the most fouled by animal excrement, to be washed and disinfected at once. I rather think that Mr Darrell, unfortunate man, may have become infected when he took off his boots on Monday night to run barefoot on blistered feet. It is through an open wound that the disease enters the body. I strongly advise you to retain your footwear at every stage of the race. If you have cuts or abrasions, have them covered. The doctors will help.'

'I'm for quitting,' Chalk said. 'Tetanus. That's something doctors can't cure.'

'That is perfectly true,' Mostyn-Smith admitted. 'But we know enough about it to take reasonable precautions. If I thought there was a real danger, I should have retired from this contest already. Of course, the decision is your own. Bear in mind that we shall not be certain until after the post-mortem examination. It may be that he died from other causes.'

He actually raised his pace a fraction to put a decent distance between them and him. They conferred for several minutes as they walked. Apparently a group decision was to be made. Then O'Flaherty detached himself and approached Mostyn-Smith again.

'You say we're not likely to catch it if we keep our feet clean?'

'Bearing in mind that you aren't likely to suffer skin damage on any other part of your person, yes. Whether Mr Darrell died from tetanus or some other cause, it is still good advice. That is why I arranged for our hut to be scrubbed, Mr O'Flaherty.'

The Irishman accepted the point in silence.

'And you're going on with this tramp yourself?'

'I fully intend to,' Mostyn-Smith affirmed. 'I shall make up the time that I lost this morning by increasing my stridelength.'

A little devilment made him add, 'If you gentlemen withdraw, I should be among the leaders by Friday.'

This reminder that Darrell's death had increased the chances of prize money tipped the scales in the pedestrians' decision to continue. After another brief consultation the group broke into a run, and trotted away in step into a faster lap to celebrate their resolve. They raised dust, defined in pale beams of sunlight that had penetrated the grimy vaulting.

Erskine Chadwick sat at lunch in his tent, watched by Harvey. The meal was cold, but well prepared, and he consumed it noisily. The morning's tragedy had not touched him. Darrell had scarcely existed, except as a yardstick. The poor fellow was dead, so Herriott would probably promote some other worthy trudger to the inner track and the race would continue. The tetanus scare had not bothered Chadwick either. That eccentric little medico from the outer path had made a point of mentioning the risk. But after army service the only risks that troubled Chadwick arose on the Stock Market.

The full blare of the band invaded the tent for an instant as the flap was drawn open. Walter Jacobson came in.

'Forgive this intrusion. I should like to speak with you about the race, and I don't wish to delay you. The matter is of some importance.'

'Please sit down, then. Our furniture is sparse, but if you don't object to sitting on the bed ...?'

Jacobson, ill at ease, fluttered his hand to decline the offer.

'To come to the point, you will have heard of Mr Darrell's tragic passing, and I think you will understand that this has thrown the whole future of the contest into uncertainty. We – that is, the management – would wish to continue with the race, providing that the participants feel able to go on.'

Chadwick felt totally able, but feigned a moment's decent hesitation.

'Of course,' he ventured, 'one feels reluctant in these unhappy circumstances ...'

'Quite, quite. Do continue your meal, won't you?'

'However, as a military man,' Chadwick added with an air of fortitude, 'I learned to accept such things philosophically. And as an athlete I have trained my body to persevere, even when the mind protests. I think that poor Darrell would wish us to continue the race.'

'I am so glad that you feel this way. I hope that your fellow-competitors are equally resolute.' Jacobson produced a large handkerchief and dusted the back of his neck. 'What we now have to settle is how we rearrange the race.'

Chadwick had prepared for this.

'Yes. There was a good deal of interest in the duel between Darrell and me.'

'We have a problem,' Jacobson continued, 'in that no single competitor seems worthy of consideration as your antagonist.'

He paused, allowing Chadwick to savour the flattery.

'If, for example, I nominated Williams, who holds second place by a small margin, he might be overtaken tomorrow by O'Flaherty, or even Chalk.'

Suspicion dawned on Chadwick's face.

'So I have come to suggest,' Jacobson said, speaking more quickly, 'that instead of making the main contest a two-man race, we alter the conditions a little so that you are challenged by all-corners – which was in real terms always the case.'

'But I do not exactly follow—'

'In other words, we dispense with one of the tracks and all competitors run on the outer path, which is wider than the other.'

Having delivered his dart, Jacobson paused to study its effect.

Chadwick picked up a knife from the plate and held it poised on his fingers, pointing at Jacobson.

'You are seriously suggesting,' he said in a voice thick with menace, 'that I appear on a track with the drunks and half-wits who are out there at the moment. Is that it, Mr Jacobson?'

'Well-known pedestrians, many of them,' Jacobson stammered.

'Clowns or criminals, every one! Perhaps you aren't aware, sir, that I hold the Queen's Commission. I am not unused to dealing with the lower levels of society. I wouldn't allow one of that rabble to clean my blasted boots!' With an air of finality he snatched an orange that Harvey was holding and bisected it savagely.

Jacobson selected his next words with care.

'So I must now inform Mr Herriott that you are retiring from the contest?'

'That is not what I said.'

'But the effect of what you said is the same, Mr Chadwick. First, you have no rival left. Second, you refuse to appear with the antagonists who are nominated. The conclusion is obvious.'

Chadwick was beginning to see he had no choice, but he continued to resist.

'Nominate Williams and I shall permit him to share my path.'

Jacobson played his ace.

'I doubt that Williams or any of his fellows would risk stepping on the inner track. The doctors' suspicion is that Mr Darrell died of tetanus, contracted when he ran bare-foot on that very path. The ground may be contaminated.'

Harvey had removed Chadwick's boots and socks for airing purposes. The naked feet, resting squarely on the stone floor, were abruptly tilted so that only the heels remained in contact.

'If I were to accept your proposal, and move to the outer path, I should expect some form of compensation. The sacrifice, you see, would be all on my side. The benefit to the promotion and its public appeal would be immeasurable.'

This was capitulation. Jacobson was delighted.

'I think you may be confident that Mr Herriott will make some recognition of this sporting gesture. Shall I suggest fifty?'

Chadwick reached for his socks.

'Suggest a hundred and I'll settle for that.'

Jacobson nodded assent and turned to leave.

'One more thing,' said Chadwick. 'You will arrange for this floor to be disinfected?'

'At once.'

Jacobson hurried away to secure Herriott's agreement. It was quickly given, and when Chadwick rejoined the race at 12.30 p.m. he started on the outer circuit behind Billy Reid, whose brother had bullied him into resuming. On the other side of the track O'Flaherty and his friends were already devising tactics to ensure that Chadwick earned every penny of his hundred pounds.

Later in the afternoon Sol Herriott was preparing a statement for the newspapers about the altered race arrangements. He sat near the starting area on a mahogany chair taken from the boardroom. The grey tip of his cigar grew, fell and disintegrated on his pinstripes. Officials prattling behind him did not break his concentration; the urgency of the task preoccupied him. If Wednesday morning's Press suggested that the promotion might collapse, the effect could be disastrous. He was composing a piece to present Chadwick's move to the second track as a sensation. The whole venture would be given an impetus.

In general, he had been pleased by the morning editions, which appeared too late to carry the news of Darrell. The careers of the main entrants were fully described, and much was made of the different backgrounds of Chadwick and Darrell. The remainder of the field had been referred to as 'the huddled-up division' – a slighting reference to their accommodation but otherwise the comments were flippant, but uncritical. Herriott had liked 'the Boss of the Hippodrome', and 'that staunch sportsman'. If tragedy had not intervened, he would have enjoyed this day.

One of the competitors, Reid, had twice tottered off course during the last hour, and fresh sawdust had been put down to mark the inner edge of the track. The rest, though, were in good shape. All of them now chose to walk, and the pace varied little from man to man. Chadwick undoubtedly showed the best form, but two knots of competitors contrived to impede him whenever he overtook. Chalk's antics in cutting across the Captain's path were hugely enjoyed, and Williams too delighted the crowd by dogging Chadwick's steps for a full lap, aping the upthrust chin.

This mood of mirth was cut short by the entrance of a woman in dark clothes, heavily veiled and accompanied by an elderly man. She crossed the track to speak to Herriott. After a word to Jacobson, who took over the Press release, Herriott led them to his office.

'It was a great shock,' he began, when they were seated.

Cora Darrell had lifted her veil.

'A wicked thing. Mr Herriott, may I introduce my father?'

'McCarthy is my name.'

He offered his hand. 'It was good of you to send word so quickly of my son-in-law's death.'

He was mildly spoken, and dressed in a faded check overcoat. Repair-stitching showed on his shoes, which he had polished to a military standard.

'I wish that we could have informed you when he first collapsed,' Herriott answered, 'but none of us suspected anything but cramp at that stage. After that, the attacks came so suddenly and so violently that we were totally taken up with his condition. The whole thing was over in less than two hours.'

'These attacks,' asked McCarthy. 'Did they become steadily worse?'

'I was not with him to the end,' Herriott answered. 'We had two doctors in attendance, and they told me that the attacks were in the nature of muscular spasms. He was conscious until the last moments.'

Cora covered her face, sobbing. Her father rested a hand on her arm.

'The doctors,' he said. 'Could I see them?'

'The doctor mainly concerned left to conduct the post-mortem examination at Islington mortuary. I shall be pleased to arrange a meeting later. The other doctor volunteered his help. He is a competitor in the race – Mostyn-Smith. If you would care to meet him—'

'Not if he is on the track at present. We should not

interrupt his running again. Did either of the doctors venture an opinion of the cause?'

'They said that tetanus was a possibility.'

'Tetanus? You don't get that running, do you? I thought it entered the body through a wound. Don't soldiers get that? I'm sure it is due to dirty wounds.'

Herriott looked down.

'I'm sorry. I know very little.'

'But I really don't understand,' McCarthy persisted. 'My son-in-law apparently died in agony from a disease that has to infect the body through a wound.'

'His feet,' faltered Herriott. 'The blisters had broken. There were cuts. He ran on the path without boots or socks.'

Cora Darrell suddenly veered from passive grief to hysterical anger.

'Cuts! Open wounds! And he ran on them, over this filthy ground! What was his trainer doing, to allow this? Where is Sam Monk? What kind of trainer is he? Oh, Charlie, Charlie, he killed you. Monk killed you.'

McCarthy, mumbling apologies, tried to calm his daughter. But she controlled herself, pushing him away.

'I demand to see Mr Monk. I am entitled to a proper explanation. Where is my husband's trainer?'

'I ... don't think you should see him today,' Herriott answered. 'Like you, Mrs ... Cora, he is in a distracted state. He could give you no proper answers.'

He remembered seeing Monk in the restaurant at lunchtime, drinking alone, and heavily. By now he would be in a stupor.

'Mr Herriott is right, my dear,' added McCarthy. 'It would serve no useful purpose.'

Cora was now calm, and spoke slowly.

'We shall sue that man, for wicked negligence. And you, Sol. We are old friends, I know, but if I can prove that you are responsible in any way for Charles's death, I shall sue. You and your ridiculous race robbed me of his love – my lawful right – for the last six weeks of his life.'

'Now, Cora,' protested her father, 'you cannot—'

'There are thousands of witnesses to the filth of this building,' she continued, ignoring him. 'Thousands, Sol. And if the law allows it, I'll prove you responsible.'

Herriott remained silent, stunned by the suddenness of the young widow's attack. Cora had said all that she wanted and stood ready to leave. Her father formed an apology on his lips but only uttered a meaningless sound. Nodding awkwardly, he motioned Cora to the door and they left Herriott alone.

That evening was not a comfortable one for Herriott. Although a fair crowd accumulated in the stands they were less animated than the band. The performers on the track gave a dreary show. Only Billy Reid provided occasional diversions by sitting, on strike, at the track edge, while his brother's appeals were taken up by those near by, 'Go it, Billy! You've got 'em all beat, my beauty. Get up, Billy boy!' – until he roused himself for another laborious circuit. Midway through the evening Sam Monk awoke from a drunken slumber in the restaurant and tottered into the arena pestering the officials for money. Herriott cast about for Jacobson, but the manager, as usual, was elsewhere, and the job of evicting Monk had to be his own.

Most of the audience had left and the pedestrians themselves were starting to retire when Jacobson reappeared. With him were two strangers.

'These gentlemen asked to meet you. They are from the police. Sergeant – er—'

'Cribb – and Police Constable Thackeray. You are Mr Herriott, manager of this show?'

'Promoter, Jacobson here is the manager.'

'Very good. I am from the Detective Branch. Here to investigate the death of Charles Frederick Darrell. Pedestrian, I believe?'

'Yes. But why—'

'Doctors' report came in tonight. He died of poisoning, sir. Enough strychnine in the corpse to put down a drayhorse. Where shall we talk?'

THE PEDESTRIAN CONTEST AT ISLINGTON

Positions at the end of the Second Day

Name	Miles	Laps
CAPT. ERSKINE CHADWICK	202	0
GEORGE WILLIAMS	196	2
FEARGUS O'FLAHERTY	196	2
PETER CHALK	187	5
DAVID STEVENS	182	4
JAMES GAFFNEY	181	0
WILLIAM REID	180	5
MONTAGUE LAWTON	179	3
WALTER HOLLAND	176	0
MATTHEW JENKINS	175	3
CHARLES JONES	174	3
FRANCIS MOSTYN-SMITH	169	4

C. Darrell (125 miles), and G. Stockwell (139 miles) retired from the race.

7

Wednesday

The boardroom still contained the bedstead which had been installed there eighteen hours earlier. It now served as a coat-rack. When he was seated Herriott offered cigars to the other three, lit one for himself (he badly needed it), and studied the policemen, envying their vitality at this late hour. Sergeant Cribb remained standing, tall, spare in frame, too spry in his movements ever to put on much weight. His head, which switched positions with a birdlike suddenness, was burdened with an overlong nose. He had compensated for this by cultivating the bushiest Piccadilly Weepers that Herriott had seen. These, and his heavy eyebrows, were deep-brown, flecked with grey. He looked in his forties.

Jacobson asked, 'What do you want us to do?'

'Do, sir? Do nothing. Talk to us. That's all.'

Cribb fastened his attention on Herriott.

'The late Mr Darrell – tell me what you can about him.'

'I can't say that I knew very much about him at all, poor

77

fellow. A first-class distance runner – I had that on expert advice, or I'd never have matched him with Chadwick. He trained uncommon hard for this race. Looked a cert when I watched him at Hackney Wick. His trainer was the best in England – Sam Monk.'

A nod to Constable Thackeray, who was busy with a notebook.

'So you take him on. Give him any cash at this stage?'

'That isn't the practice. The prize money is generous enough. If Darrell won he would net five hundred, plus sidestakes.'

'And if he didn't?'

'A hundred for second place. Fifty for third. The opposition didn't amount to much.'

Cribb paused, while his assistant, a burly, middle-aged man with a fine grey beard, caught up with his note-taking.

'This newspaper.' He produced a copy of that day's *Star*. 'Read it?'

'Some of it.'

'The report on your affair?'

'Yes. I read that.'

'Substantially correct?' asked Cribb.

The pace of his questioning was straining Herriott, who faltered. The question was flashed at Jacobson.

'The details are right, yes. Some of the allusions to Mr Herriott—'

'No matter. Darrell takes the lead after six hours. Right?'

'Yes.'

'Chadwick falls behind, and takes to running?'

Jacobson nodded.

'Not much resting till twenty-four hours are up?'

'Only for light meals.'

'Darrell's wife – says here she visits him. He doesn't stop?'

It seemed a very long time ago. Herriott took over the answers.

'I showed Mrs Darrell around the arena. She didn't want to interfere with the running.'

'You show her around? She wants to see his tent, I expect?'

'I simply introduced her to some of the officials. She knows most of us. We didn't look into Darrell's tent.'

Jacobson remembered. 'Monk – that's Herriott's trainer – took Mrs Darrell in there.'

The eyebrows jerked higher. 'For long?'

'Oh, not much longer than five minutes.'

Constable Thackeray, finding the standing position awkward for writing, sat on the bed.

'Then she leaves?'

'As far as I can remember, yes.'

Cribb ran his finger down the newspaper which he was holding.

'The last hour. Darrell in poor shape. Foxing, is he?'

'Oh, I don't think so,' Jacobson answered. 'His feet were troubling him. He took off his running shoes before the end. Several of the runners were limping.'

'Monk attends him, I suppose? Gets him back in the tent at one o'clock?'

'Yes. Most of the competition chose to rest at that stage.'

'Now then.' Cribb had dissected the report to his

satisfaction, and tossed the paper in Thackeray's direction. 'Darrell comes out again. What time?'

'Soon after four.'

'How's he looking?'

'Very good at that stage,' Herriott recalled. 'He set off at a clinking pace. The feet seemed to have improved a lot.'

'Erratic?'

'I don't think so. He seemed well in command, but full of energy.'

Cribb's face lit into a momentary smile.

'Not surprising. Full of strychnine. Acts as a stimulant. The first spasm, now. When does that come?'

'That would have been about six.'

'Six. Is it now? Thought it might come earlier. Maybe the running makes a difference. Must check that.'

He patted the tip of his nose several times with his index finger.

'Time of death? No matter. I've got that.'

Herriott took the opportunity of a lull in the interrogation to raise a point that was troubling him deeply.

'Sergeant, this investigation. Does it mean that you will want me to cancel the race?'

'Cancel? Whatever for? Keep it going, Mr Herriott. Keep it going as long as you can. Perfect for investigating a poisoning. Everyone's here, you see. Might ask you to extend it into next week if I'm held up.'

Neither Jacobson nor Herriott was equal at this hour to the sergeant's style of humour, so he turned to other matters.

'This man Monk. He's the cove I've got to see.'

80

'You won't learn too much from him,' commented Herriott. 'The man is drunk. He took to the bottle this afternoon, drinking alone. He seemed to be doing it with the idea of getting stoned out of his mind. He fell into a stupor eventually, and then woke up and made a scene out there in the arena. I hauled him over to a spare hut. He's sleeping it off there.'

'We'll have him out, then. Must grill him at once. Get him sobered up and bring him to Darrell's tent. I'll see him there.'

Herriott had hoped for a chance to sleep after the questioning, but clearly he and Jacobson had been co-opted as members of the Detective Branch. Sergeant Cribb's tone stifled protest.

'Another thing,' he snapped. 'The second doctor, Mostyn-Smith. Hook him out of bed. We'll hear his story while you dowse Monk.'

'Mostyn-Smith won't be in bed,' said Jacobson. 'He doesn't normally rest for more than a half-hour. They say he gets his best walking done when the rest are sleeping. After this morning he'll have a long stretch to make up.'

Cribb was not inconsiderate quite to the point of brutality.

'Lost some ground, did he? Can't have him losing more, then. How long since you finished beat-bashing, Thackeray?'

The constable returned the look of a trapped bear.

'Three years, Sarge. The feet, you know.'

'Splendid. Should hold you up for a mile. Get out there with the Doc. You know the line of questioning.

81

Not a word about the strychnine. We'll keep that close at present. Understood, gents? Off you go, then.' He passed each of the others his coat, and then tested the mattress of Darrell's death-bed, heaved his long legs on to it and reclined there.

'I'll have that cigar before you go, Mr Herriott,' he said.

The gas had been turned down soon after midnight, perhaps to encourage competitors to retire for their short sleep, and so release the late shift of officials. By one-fifteen, only Mostyn-Smith, his long-suffering lap-scorer and a somnolent judge slumped in his chair occupied the arena. When the light in Chadwick's tent was extinguished, the stunted blue flames on the chandeliers gave the scene a positively gloomy aspect. The little walker, at times hardly distinguishable in his black costume, strode busily around the white-edged circuit, as though performing some gnomic ritual.

Constable Edward Thackeray was not a man to be troubled by atmospheres, sinister or otherwise. His long career in the Force was blemished here and there by other short-comings, but in situations that required a steady pulse he was exemplary. It had become accepted in every station at which he served (he was often moved) that Thackeray was the constable who attended the most gruesome occasions; he was a tower of strength at exhumations. This gift unhappily did not bring the promotion that he once expected, but it had, early in 1878, brought him on to the fringe of a murder investigation, leading to the arrest of the notorious Charles Peace. The formation of the

Detective Branch soon afterwards, and the call for constables experienced in serious crimes, led to Thackeray's present appointment. He was justly proud.

He approached the track and watched the solitary pedestrian for a full lap, assessing the rate of progress as a cautious swimmer tests the water. At length he recognized Cribb's brisk step somewhere behind him, and this encouraged him to cross the arena to await Mostyn-Smith on the track itself. He stepped smartly away at the right moment, pace for pace with the walker, exchanged identities and then gave all his attention to the walk. The rate of progress was not excessive, but he found that to maintain it comfortably he had to swing his arms across his chest. That, in ulster and bowler-hat, embarrassed him a little. Somewhere in the shadows Cribb would be savouring the spectacle.

At length, inhibitions conquered, he opened the questioning.

'You are the doctor who attended the man that died?'

'I assisted. The official doctor was always in charge of the patient,' answered Mostyn-Smith, speaking without strain.

'You was with him till the end, though?'

'Yes, that is true.'

'What we need to know, Doctor, is whether he made statements of any sort while you attended him.'

There was a pause while they passed close to the lap-scorer.

'Not strictly statements,' Mostyn-Smith said. 'The spasms were set off by the slightest movement, you see. Although he was fully conscious, we tried to discourage him from speech, even early in the condition. He did, however, make it clear, by the briefest utterances, that he could not understand the reason for his condition.'

'What was they, sir?'

Thackeray instinctively felt for his notebook, thought again, and let it drop back into the pocket.

'Oh, odd fragments. I remember that he said, "Never happened to me before." And later, "What causes this?" Otherwise they were mostly exclamations of pain.'

The constable inhaled a gulp of air, committing the phrases to memory.

'Did you give the man anything to drink?'

'Warm tea, Officer. It sometimes helps.'

'Nobody else visited the room, I suppose?'

'Nobody else.'

'Thank you, sir. You didn't know Mr Darrell before the race?'

'Not at all.'

'I think that's all then, sir. You carrying on like this for long?'

'Until Saturday. Good night to you.'

Thackeray eased his stride, and Mostyn-Smith padded cheerfully away into the gloom. The constable raised a leg and massaged his aching shin. At Cribb's voice, immediately behind him, he dropped it like a guardsman.

'Watch it, Thackeray. Next event the high jump.'

A bleak smile greeted the sergeant.

'Right, then. What did you get while you were footing it?'

Just as you thought, Sarge. Victim said very little, but enough to put suicide out of the question.'

They approached Darrell's tent. Thackeray was moving forward to open the flap, when Cribb restrained him, raising a hand for silence. With the stealth of a brave he crept to the opening, loosened the flap and flung it open. Someone inside scrambled to his feet. It was a uniformed policeman.

'Never rest on duty,' Cribb advised him. 'I might have held a knife, lad.'

The young constable sheepishly emerged to face a withering look from Thackeray. Cribb dismissed him to the Hall's police office where the detectives had first swooped on him as he was drinking cocoa, earlier in the evening.

With the lamp ignited, Darrell's tent made a passable interviewing room. As well as two chairs and a bedside table, which Thackeray at once rearranged, there was a gas-ring and kettle. Milk and a teapot were found in a small food-cupboard, which also contained bread, whisky, a tin of liniment, various potions, a leathery remnant of calf-bladder and a slice of strong-smelling cod. Still on the table were the bottle and mug from which Darrell had taken Monk's 'bracer'. Cribb sniffed at them charily and removed them to the cupboard.

'We'll have every liquid analyzed,' he announced. 'Your job, Thackeray. Get 'em out at daybreak to a lab. Now where's this trainer? Monk ... Monk; heard of him, have you?'

'Can't say that I have, Sarge. But that doesn't mean a lot. On my earnings I ain't what you'd call one of the Fancy.'

'Just as well,' Cribb reassured him. 'But if you ever do lay a bet, remember this: four legs support a body better than two. I'll trade foot-racing for a Newmarket sweep any day.'

85

There was the sound outside of scuffled footsteps. Walter Jacobson entered, half-supporting Sam Monk, a bedraggled figure, damp about the head and shoulders. He deposited him in the waiting chair. He was about to seat himself on the still unmade bed when Cribb intervened.

'My thanks, sir. And now you – and Mr Herriott' (the promoter had just heralded his entry by kicking a hip bath) 'shall get some sleep. Busy day coming up, I dare say.'

After their exit, Thackeray fastened the flap and took a standing position behind Monk, resting his weight on the chair-back. The flickering light greatly magnified his shadow so that it loomed over the trainer like a shade from hell. It was not his intention to terrorize the man. He was there merely to see that Monk did not relapse into sleep. The worst that threatened was a timely prod.

'Your name Monk?' Cribb began, without much refinement.

'Yes.'

'You know who we are? Police officers.'

A wary glint in his eye showed that the point had not escaped Monk.

'Making inquiries into the death of Charles Darrell.'

A pause, while Cribb studied his man.

'You're fit to talk, are you?'

'Yes,' answered Monk without enthusiasm.

'Known him long, then?'

'Two year, off and on.'

'And took over his training . . . ?'

'December, seventy-seven. He managed himself up to then.'

86

'You made a better runner of him, though?'

Monk was not easily deceived by flattery.

'He knew the game well enough before he met me.'

'Never took such big prizes, though.'

Cribb's brief study of Darrell's career was helpful. The praise loosened Monk's tongue a little.

'I taught him a bit. We was a good partnership, me and Charlie. He would have won this mix, no doubt of that. Bloody tragic, this is.'

'You prepared him well, then?'

'Never better. When Charlie toed the scratch last Sunday night he was set for six hundred. No doubt of it.'

Cribb shifted suddenly to the attack.

'What went wrong, then?'

'What d'you mean, mister?'

'The man was limping by Monday night. That's no champion.'

'Ah, foot trouble. Nought you can do about that. Blisters. I had 'em fixed, though. Likely he looked worse than he was. Charlie could be tricky, you know.'

'Right! Tuesday morning, one o'clock. He comes in here to sleep. What state is he in?'

The switch of tense and the sudden reminder where they were proved effective. From Monk's expression it was clear that the scene flashed vividly into his mind's eye.

'Worried about them blisters. I said I'd fix them before he ran again, and then he was more content.'

'He doesn't eat anything, or take a drink?'

'Not then. You see he'd taken the odd hunk of bread as he walked. All he needed was sleep.'

87

'Right. So what do you do then?'

'Me? Why, I left him, once he was comfy.'

'And then?'

'He slept.'

'And you?'

Monk's eyes took on an opaque glaze.

'I passed the time till he woke.'

'How?' The point was not to be evaded.

'With a friend.'

'In here?'

'No. Finsbury Park. I took a cab. I were back by four, when Charlie needed to wake.'

'Lady?'

Monk confirmed the fact with a twitch of his features.

'Look, you can't need her name. It ain't important,' he appealed.

Out of his sight Thackeray removed one hand from the chairback and raised an inquiring eyebrow at Cribb. A nudge was imminent, but Cribb gave no consenting nod.

'We'll leave her out of it for now. May need the name later, mind.'

He allowed Monk to relax, coaxing him out of his defensive stand.

'It's coming up to four, then, and you go back to the Hall. Straight to Darrell?'

He tried to remember.

'I think ... yes, I drank a coffee first, and talked to Chadwick's trainer.'

'Small-talk?'

'Well, yes, trainers' talk. I tried to get him to come to

terms on an easy second day, but he wouldn't. It would have helped Charlie's feet, you see. Chadwick was a sight groggy on his pins after running, and I thought he'd see the sense of it.'

'You didn't wrangle over it?'

'Oh no. I got back to Charlie to wake him sharp at four.'

'With a drink?' The query was slipped in, almost disinterestedly.

'I gave him a drop of something, yes.'

'That would be this.' Cribb reached to the cupboard and took out the bottle. 'What's in it?'

Monk shot a suspicious glance at the sergeant.

'It's a kind of tonic. I make it myself, from sugar, brandy and liquorice. Helps them to stir themselves, you see. Every ped takes a bracer now and then.'

Cribb took a sniff at the liquid. Sediment at the base clouded the contents as the bottle was moved.

'What else is there in this?'

'That's all,' Monk said.

Without any warning, Cribb snatched at Monk's throat, grasped his muffler and pulled him forward.

'What else?'

The lamp above them, jerked by the movement, sent their shadows leaping about the tent.

'I don't—'

Constable Thackeray leaned over Monk, his face so close that his beard rasped the trainer's ear.

'Speak up!'

'Stimulants,' Cribb breathed at him. 'Stimulants. We're not green, Monk.'

89

The grip tightened.

'All right, yes. I give him a crystal.'

'Of what?'

'Some chemical. It never did no harm to him. I swear that.'

'What chemical?'

'The usual – strychnine. It livens up a man wonderful.'

There was something in the naivety of Monk's answer that made Cribb relax his hold.

'You've used strychnine before?'

'Used it for years. I took it myself in my time. Small doses, mind.'

Cribb sat back in his chair, beating a tattoo with his boot as he weighed the effect of what had been said. Here was a complication – a development that irritated and intrigued him. He ought to have remembered that sportsmen, the real professionals who engaged in endurance contests, whether in pedestrianism, pugilism or the new craze of bicycling, were known to take stimulants. Vegetable alkaloids like atropine and strychnine, if taken in minute amounts, would revitalize flagging muscles.

He picked up the bottle.

'How much strychnine in here?'

'Enough to make a tired man nimble. I crushed a crystal and used half the powder.'

'And how much of this did Darrell drink?'

Monk reflected.

'He had a second mug. Well, you can see. The bottle was full up to there.'

'And this was the only lot he took?'

90

'That's so.'

The sergeant paused again, studying Monk's reactions, judging whether his calm was due to sluggishness, the alcohol in his veins, or whether he had rehearsed himself for questions like this.

'I'll speak plainly, Monk. You're in trouble. This could be manslaughter, and if it is, I'll have you.'

For the first time, genuine alarm showed in the trainer's eyes.

'You can't get me for that! It's not true. You can't nail a man for a bloody illness! Tetanus ain't my doing, no more than yours.'

Cribb opened the cupboard and replaced the bottle there.

'Ever heard of artificial tetanus?'

'What?'

'Artificial tetanus, Monk. That's what killed Darrell. Strychnine poisoning.'

The trainer's face twitched with shock, repeatedly.

Cribb continued: 'The body of the man you livened up with strychnine was opened earlier today. Specimens were taken – fluids from the body. You understand? Some was fed to a rat. It was convulsed in minutes, and died very soon after. That man's body contained strychnine, Monk. Not small amounts. Not half a powdered crystal. A massive dose. You tipped it in like sugar, did you?'

Monk was shaking his head, incapable of words.

Cribb persisted. 'Where d'you buy it?'

'Bethnal Green. Hayward – small chemist there.'

'How much?'

91

'Five crystals. No more, I swear it. I paid heavy for that.'

'I don't doubt it. You signed for it?'

'Yes.'

'Where's the rest, then?'

'In my room. I lodge at Hackney Wick. It's in a phial there. That's where I made up the bracer. Believe me, mister.'

'We don't need to. We can check. Address?'

'Rupert Street. 118.'

'Got that, Thackeray? Now, Monk. I want this straight. You're telling us what's in that bottle is not enough to kill a man. You gave him two mugfuls—'

'He asked for the second.'

'You gave him two. He drank nothing else?'

'Nor ate a thing. God's truth.'

'You're sure of this? We'll get this down for you to sign. You made no mistake in mixing the liquid?'

'None. I done it careful.'

'I hope so for your sake. We'll get it analyzed in the morning. One other thing. When did you bring the bottle into the Hall?'

'Sunday night. Same day as I made the stuff. We was allowed in at ten to inspect the tents and dump our baggage.'

'Where did you put the bottle?'

'In the cupboard with the other stuff.'

'So it was there till the next night, when you took it out to revive Darrell?'

'Yes.'

There was no longer any hint of incoherence about

Monk. The realization of his position had honed his reactions to razor sharpness.

Sergeant Cribb got to his feet. For the first time he spoke slowly, enunciating each word.

'We'll check what you've said. I hope it's gospel truth. Frankly, Monk, I know enough to hold you on suspicion of manslaughter. What I'll do instead is ask you to stay in this building until I tell you otherwise. You've been given a hut to sleep in, have you?'

'Some of the boys gave up in the first twenty-four hours. Mr Herriott put me in a spare hut. I could ask to stay there.'

'Good. Get back to bed then. Keep off the liquor. There's ways of sobering a man that act quicker than cold water. Don't forget that. And don't try leaving the Hall. I've men on the doors.' There were always police on duty at the Hall's functions, but Cribb emphasized the point as though they had been brought in to act as warders for Monk.

Without speaking, Monk left the tent.

Thackeray, stiff after his exercise, took the vacant chair. Cribb sat on the bed, removing his boots.

'How's the time?'

There was a music hall joke that constables on the beat, used to dealing with drunks in dark streets, acquired handsome watches early in their careers. Thackeray referred to his gold half-hunter.

'Three o'clock near enough, Sarge.'

'Good. There's time to write the statement before you take this lot away for testing. I saw pen and ink in the police office. You can check that the man there's awake.' He raised his legs on to the bed and yawned. 'Turn out the lamp before you go.'

Thackeray, wrestling with his private thoughts about a policeman's lot, extinguished the flame. Before leaving, he addressed Cribb again.

'In the morning, Sarge, when I'm back from the lab – who do we see next?'

'Depends on the results. We have to find how he took the strychnine. Anyway, I must look up the man's widow. I'll do that before you get back.'

'She's been told?'

'Oh yes. Told he's dead. Thinks it was tetanus. Poor woman's got a shock coming.' He turned over in bed, yawning again. 'Wake me at four. I'll have a coffee. For God's sake watch what goes into it.'

8

At four on Wednesday morning the lights were turned up and a bell was rung. This reveille had been arranged by Sol Herriott, before leaving for 'a decent eight hours' in a hotel nearby. Already, in near-darkness at the Liverpool Road end, loyal friends and trainers were moving about the area of the huts, rousing their inhabitants. Their method of restoring consciousness had been well proved in other institutions. The door was thrust open. Blankets were yanked from resisting hands. In hard cases the dripping cold sponge was employed. Soon, to a chorus of protesting obscenities, the huts themselves were illuminated. The ministering angels flitted among them, bearing away buckets that steamed in the night air, returning for milk from the communal churn, igniting the gas-rings, and all the time growling deterrents to further sleep.

After clearing their tins of groats and broth, and submitting to painful reunions with their boots, the slit-eyed champions hobbled, stiff and shivering, towards the arena. Billy Reid led the parade; his brother made sure of that. Gaffney and Lawton, two silent northerners who had survived so far, but without threatening the others, followed. Reid's wily co-tenant, looking the freshest of the bunch, was just ahead of the final trio, Chalk, Williams and O'Flaherty, who were discussing tactics.

'Chadwick wants nobblin',' Williams was suggesting, 'and it wants to be when there ain't no crowd about. 'E's on our bloody track now. We're soft as cheese if we don't fix the bugger.'

'You can't,' O'Flaherty told him. 'There's too many eyes on him all the time, mate. You'd be out of the race before you'd lifted your boot. That trainer of his never moves from the track. And there's too many of the Fancy with a good book on Chadwick now that Darrell's gone. They'd do bloody murder to you.'

'Not if we got 'im now, before first light.'

'No chance. I tell you the trainer sees everything. Now look at the crowd there already – clockers, lapmen, bloody Jacobson. We'd best keep it straight, I say. Warm it up for him. He might strain a sinew.'

The Half-breed spat contemptuously.

'That bugger ain't crackin' unless we stop 'im.'

Chalk now intervened.

'Yes, you fix 'im this mornin' and what bloody 'appens? I tell you. They call off the bloody show, and you and me get blistered dogs for nothing. Don't be so soft. They'd never keep the race going another four days for us to scoop the bloody pool. If Chadwick goes before Saturday so do the rest of us.'

There was a convincing ring to this argument, and Williams lapsed into gloomy silence.

'Good sleep, Feargus?' Chalk airily continued.

'Better than the first night. The smell of carbolic gets into me, though. Stops me breathing right.'

'Did you see Double-barrel?'

'Not at all. I don't think he'd dare come near while I'm there. I'm going to pole-axe the little devil when I catch him. What sort of doctor is he, anyway? Tetanus, says he, and gets every hut scrubbed so's you can't exercise your nostrils decently. Then when it's all done and stinking like the workhouse they tell us Darrell died of the poison. Doctor? I shouldn't wonder if he dosed the man with strychnine himself. Look at him there now. Can you see that in frock-coat and spats?'

They watched Mostyn-Smith, red-faced and shaggy bearded, complete another circuit in his eccentric style. It was indeed difficult to visualize him sitting dignified in a doctor's gig, visiting the sick.

As the pedestrians reached the track they signalled to the lap-takers that they were ready. Erskine Chadwick left his tent suitably groomed (he was the one man in the race who was shaved each morning) and looking deceptively alert in freshly laundered kit. Only when he took up his starting stance automatically on the inner track was his tiredness betrayed. Raucous reminders from his fellow-travellers caused Harvey, who was also yawning, to re-route the Captain. By the time he had caught a lap-taker's eye he was the last to get away.

Sergeant Cribb at about this time fell victim to his own efficiency. He had been awakened at four exactly by Thackeray, bearing a coffee made as he liked it, with a mere trace of milk and sugar. It was his plan to spend an hour in bed reviewing Monk's statement and deciding how the investigation should proceed. But Thackeray returned with a crate from the police office and began noisily packing it with the contents of the food cupboard. When the job was completed, Cribb's concentration was shattered. Resignedly, he reached for his boots.

'Finished, then? Hump the stuff back to the office. We'll get some breakfast if they serve it here. Restaurant's near the office.'

'I've got to get to the lab at Saville Street, Sarge.'

'That's easily done. I've to see the widow. Drop you off on the way.'

Cribb was obliged to wait in the hall of the Darrell residence at Finsbury Park. Mrs Darrell, the servant told him, would not be a few moments. Twelve minutes later (he cynically tested her estimate on the watch) he was shown into the morning-room. Cora Darrell was seated in an upright armchair, sewing a black veil on to a hat. Formalities were exchanged. Cribb expressed his sympathy.

'Sorry to disturb you, too. Visitors aren't wanted at these times. However—'

As though she shared his wish to get to the point, Cora interrupted:

'It's that man Monk, isn't it? He has been to you, has he? I thought he might, when he heard I was taking a lawyer's advice. Well, it makes no difference, no difference at all. We shall prepare a case and sue for negligence. It isn't only the loss of my husband, tragic as that is. There is money – a great deal of money involved. Except for Monk and his disgusting carelessness, we should have been richer by almost a thousand pounds. What does he hope to gain by speaking to you people? I shan't say anything, you know.'

A comment crossed Cribb's mind. In other circumstances he might have made it. Before the thought shifted, Cora began again.

'It isn't a police matter, anyway. The man failed in his duty as a trainer. Have you seen the newspapers? He allowed my Charles to run barefoot around that disgraceful track. That was inviting tetanus. How could Charles have realized the danger, after twenty-four hours of running? It was Monk's *job*, and he failed. If I get nothing back in compensation I'll still see that he never works as a trainer again. Do they have licences, that can be taken away?'

'I think you should hear what I have to say,' Cribb replied. 'The reason I came – it wasn't tetanus, madam. The tests last night showed up something else. Your husband died of strychnine poisoning.'

Cribb's statement stunned her into silence. For a moment he thought she would faint. He looked round for the bell-rope, but her colour returned.

'I cannot begin to understand. You mean he ate—'

'Or drank, ma'am. We are testing all the food and drink in the tent.'

She drew in her breath, seizing on a conclusion.

'This is wicked! Wicked! That trainer killed my husband! It's worse now, far worse. He had the feeding of Charles. Nobody else touched the food. Poison, you say. Did he let poison get into the food that Charles ate? I thought it was dangerous, the stuff he gave him. Charles wouldn't admit it, oh no. Everybody took some, he said.'

'What do you mean, Mrs Darrell?'

'Drinks to restore their strength – dangerous drinks. You know it's the practice among pedestrians to take them. Oh, I warned Charles, but what was the use? If Monk only once made a mistake – he drinks heavily, you know – it could turn a tonic into a fatal dose. You've talked to him, have you? I suppose he denies it. I shall sue him, though. Criminal negligence – that's what it is. I shall see my solicitor.'

'You knew Mr Monk had prepared something for your husband to drink during the race?'

'Well, yes. It was his practice.'

'Your husband. He was content to leave this to Monk?'

Cora's bitterness was turning to remorse. She dabbed at her eyes with a lace handkerchief.

'So often I asked him to be careful.'

'Had he taken strychnine on other occasions?'

'Well, yes. He was a professional, Sergeant. He ran for large amounts of money. If he wanted to compete on level terms with the others he had to resort to similar aids. The whole thing terrified me – I couldn't sleep for worrying – but I couldn't stop him. He always said it only made him feel better. If it hurt, he would stop.'

Another tear trickled down.

'How long had he been taking this stuff?'

'He only took it in long-distance races. The first time was in Manchester, two years ago. Since then he must have run in a dozen really long races.'

Now that her emotional outburst had subsided, Mrs

Darrell was becoming coherent. Cribb needed more information.

'If the trainer was to blame,' he said, 'I need to know why. Why so clumsy this time? Man's got a reputation. Best trainer in England, he's said to be. Should know about tonics. Why should he go wrong this time?'

'I only know that he drinks more than he should.'

'Tipped in too much when he'd been on the beer? Possible. We're having the bottle tested, of course.' He tapped his chin pensively. 'Now suppose Monk didn't make any mistake. Your husband wasn't suicidal, was he?'

'Goodness no!' Cora exclaimed in indignation, taking this as a personal slur. 'Charles had everything to live for. A successful career, happy marriage, a fortune to be won.'

'No debts, then? Have to ask, you see.'

'No debts,' she repeated, coolly.

'And his state of mind when the race started?'

'He was confident of winning. Monk had worked him hard. I've never known him so well-prepared.'

'Makes it even stranger that Mr Monk should slip up, doesn't it? Now I see from the newspaper that you visited the Hall Monday afternoon. Made quite a stir, by this account.'

Cora blushed with pleasure, clearly wondering which paper Cribb had read. She couldn't really ask him.

'Yes, I wanted to watch Charles. He was running very well. I'm sure he wasn't worried by anything.'

'You spoke to him?'

'No. Not to Charles. He was running, you see. I wasn't there to interrupt his performance.'

'You did speak to Mr Monk, I believe.'

'Yes.' She had coloured again, only slightly, but Cribb noticed. 'He showed me the living arrangements.'

'You haven't always been opposed to Mr Monk?'

She had recovered her poise.

'I was civil to the man. I asked to see the tent. I wanted to be sure it was comfortable.'

'Of course,' said Cribb. 'And was it?'

He had not forgotten his own short retirement in the tent. But he, too, could be evasive when it suited him.

'I was impressed by the accommodation.'

'Tell me, Mrs Darrell,' Cribb asked. 'Was there any bottle or container visible in the tent?'

'None – except when I asked to see the cupboard. There were a number of bottles in there. I noticed the one that Monk uses for his tonic – a large green one.'

'Oh, you did? What time would this have been?'

'I can't really recall. It must have been about four o'clock.'

'Mr Monk – was he acting normally?'

'As far as I know, yes.'

Cribb got to his feet.

'Well, Mrs Darrell. Thank you for your help. I'm sorry that my news was distressing. We're making tests to discover how he got the poison. I can let you know—'

'You are so kind.' Cora rang for the maid. 'One other matter, Sergeant. My husband's personal things – his watch, his cuff-links and things. I wouldn't want them to be lost.'

'No worry, ma'am,' Cribb reassured her. 'There are

constables guarding the tent. No one goes in there but me or my assistant.'

'Then I could collect these things?'

'If you wish. Otherwise I could put them in the office.'

'I shall come this afternoon.' She spoke decisively.

'Begging your pardon, I should make it this evening if you can, ma'am. If you get there quite late there should be no crowds. You won't want to be bothered by extra publicity. The newspaper people would pester you. Best about ten, if you can get someone to drive you down to Islington.'

'You are right, of course. I shall come late, as you suggest.'

'I'll tell my man to expect you. May be around myself.'

The maid, who had entered with Cribb's overcoat, hat and umbrella, was surprised by a theatrical wink from Cribb, out of her mistress's view, as he made the last remark. She returned a half-smothered smile and handed him the coat.

When the morning-room door was closed on Cora, and the maid stood in the hallway with Cribb he winked again, and pointed a thumb at the door.

'Keeps you busy, answering doors, does she? Plenty of visitors?'

A second less disguised giggle told Cribb what he suspected.

'When the master's in training, eh?'

A hand flew to her mouth and suppressed more laughter. In the narrow passage as she opened the door Cribb nudged her gently in the ribs.

'When's your night off?'

'Monday – night before last.'

The girl sounded despondent, but Cribb, with the information he wanted, gave a third broad wink, took his umbrella and bowler, and stepped away down the street.

9

Constable Thackeray, brisk and important, strode through the afternoon crowd gathering at the turnstiles. He nodded curtly to the uniformed policeman on duty and was admitted through the 'officials only' gate. Without cutting his stride in the least he marched to the stand entrance, was recognized by an official and waved on. Across the tracks he stepped, without a glance at the entertainment being provided. He was the bearer of news. The morning had been dull, even humiliating. While brown-coated scientists had toyed with their apparatus, testing the contents of the crate, Thackeray had been compelled to sit, waiting outside, unfit to be admitted to their researches. Now he was elevated; nobody in that Hall had the information that he did.

The sergeant was standing alone at one end of the central area, observing the race. Thackeray crunched to a too-formal halt a yard away. He moved his right arm through the beginning of a salute, and then, collecting himself, snapped it down again. Cribb continued to look in the other direction.

'Defeats me,' he said, as much to himself as the constable, 'what makes a man watch these antics. Sport? Not racing thoroughbreds, this bunch, now are they? A lame cove limping round in boots ain't poetry in motion, to my eyes.'

Thackeray coughed meaningfully. Cribb turned his eyes briefly to him and then back to the race. The walkers, mostly old troupers, were giving a restrained matinee performance.

'Could be the chink of coin, I suppose. Plenty of betting men here. But six days! I like a result in five minutes, no more. When you back a runner, Thackeray, see he's got a tail. And if that tail ain't straight in the wind as he runs, the race is too long. Remember that. You've not backed any of this lot, have you?' Thackeray shook his head, too preoccupied with his news to take this conversation further.

'How d'you get on, then?' Cribb inquired, as though the reason for Thackeray's air of urgency had just entered his brain. 'How's the Bunsen and beaker brigade? You got 'em hopping about, I hope.'

Thackeray banished small-talk with his confidential tone.

'The strychnine, Sarge. It was all in the bottle.'

'Monk's bracer?'

'All in that. Enough to kill Darrell and a dozen more. He must have ladled in the stuff, they said.'

'What about the food? Anything there?'

'None at all, Sarge. And none in the other bottles.'

'They definitely confirm strychnine?'

106

'A large amount, they told me. More than Monk said he bought. Darrell stood no chance after one mugful.'

'Hm. Looks bad for Monk. Widow threatens to sue as well. We'll keep this close. You've spoken to no one?'

Thackeray jerked his head upwards like an affronted cockerel.

'Not a living soul.'

'Very good. Now, Constable. There's more important work to be done. We must check Monk's statement. That chemist – Hayward of Bethnal Green. I want you to see him. Find out what he sold Monk. Ask to see the book. Check the signature. Ask when he sold strychnine to Monk before, and how much. And Thackeray . . . '

'Sergeant?'

'Treat him gentle. Man might lie if he thinks he's in deep.'

'I will, Sarge.'

'When you've done that,' Cribb continued, 'go to Monk's lodging-house. You'll need to see him first. Get the key. Write yourself a pass for him to sign. Whatever's necessary. Find the phial of strychnine and bring it back. Search the room for more. Thorough, mind. Could have hidden it. He hasn't the look of a Charlie Peace, but we have to check. Any bottle, empty or not, we'll have for analysis. Got all that?'

Thackeray nodded, hoping that he had.

'When shall I report, Sarge?'

'Time you've done that lot, better be tomorrow. I'm staying on here an hour and that's enough. Need to know who backs these wobblers. Interrogation, Thackeray.

Patient questioning. After that I'll be ready for a sleep. Never felt so tired.'

'In here tomorrow?' asked Thackeray.

'This very spot, and early. Have to tackle the trainer again. Shake his story a bit if we can. You get off now, and look him up. Last I heard he was in the bar.'

Thackeray headed at a conscientious rate in that direction, while Cribb ambled to the enclosure where the bookmakers had their stands, among sellers of oranges, pies and humbugs. The afternoon was a slack period. Some bookies had reserved their spaces, and would return in the evening. Several though stood idly in small groups facing the crowd, who waited, like them, for the evening.

Cribb approached a pair who looked the senior representatives present. He had recognized the shorter man, a stout, rubicund character, with a fine growth of whiskers about the mouth and chin.

'The Major, ain't it?' Cribb exclaimed. 'Never thought to see you off the turf. What's up – gees not paying these days?'

For a second there was hesitation. Then the bookie raised a finger in salute.

'Of course! Wally Cribb! Sharpest crusher in London! What's your fancy then, Sergeant? What say one of these prime beasts to beat Chadwick?' He jerked his head in the direction of O'Flaherty and Chalk, then indulging in a whimsical jog for a few laps. 'Give you good odds against the Irishman.'

Cribb was shaking his head.

'You know me better than that, Major. If they paid me enough I might find the stake for a likely nag at Epsom or Newmarket. Not for a bunion Derby, though. No, I'm here on business. If I weren't, I wouldn't be in Islington, I promise you.'

'Checking licences, are you?' inquired the second bookie, warily.

'That's not a sergeant's job,' his friend enlightened him. 'No, Cribby'll be checking on the party that died. And don't ask him about it. He won't talk. What *can* we do for you, Sergeant?'

'Charles Darrell,' announced Cribb, with such emphasis that he could have been a court usher. 'The pedestrian. Backed himself, had he?'

'Don't they all? He got in early at a good price. Stood to net five hundred if he won. Confident, he must have been, or soft-headed. A man who stakes a hundred usually hedges some of it.'

'So he really thought he'd win,' mused Cribb. 'What happened to the odds when you knew he was dead?'

'Made a bloody mockery of 'em, Sergeant, if you'll excuse the term. What odds can we offer on Chadwick now? He was favourite to start with. Now it's a fiver to a gooseberry. You won't get any odds at all on him from these lads – not unless he breaks down or takes a fit. Man's got ten miles in hand. Look at him.'

Chadwick passed near to them, certainly making sound progress, and walking more stylishly than any of his rivals.

'Is he well-backed?' asked Cribb.

'Oh yes. There's plenty who stand to scoop a tidy sum

when the soldier wins, himself included. There were some pretty bets made on Monday, when Darrell got ahead, I can tell you. Willy here took seventy to forty from Chadwick's trainer, didn't you, mate?' Willy nodded glumly.

'Darrell looked good, you see,' the 'Major' continued. 'And the touts had watched his breathings at the Wick. Chadwick had to be favourite on his known form, but Darrell looked a clinker at four to one. Then off goes Darrell on Sunday night like a dog after aniseed, and Chadwick's odds began to lengthen. That's when the fast boys like Harvey got their stake on.'

'And Chadwick himself? Does he stand to win anything?'

'Runs into three figures, I've heard. Not that I took anything from him, thank the Lord. Yes, come Saturday night, Captain. Chadwick will stand on velvet. Now how about Mostyn-whatsit at five hundred to one? Can I tempt you with that?'

'You can't,' smiled Cribb. 'I wonder why you stay here. There's not much left in this affair for you lads. Unless one of the second-raters steps out sharpish, that is. What sort of business can you do?'

The 'Major' smiled.

'Side-bets, Sergeant, side-bets. Hazard a guess now. Who covered most miles in the first twelve hours today?'

'Chadwick, I suppose.'

'And there you'd lose your stake. O'Flaherty's the boy.'

'Really? Shows how cute I am to hold back. Any other heavy bets on Chadwick, besides his own?'

'Couldn't say.'

'How about the management? Mr Herriott stand to recoup anything?'

'I wouldn't know, Sergeant. He doesn't deal with the likes of us, anyway. We're small men.'

'Jacobson?' persisted Cribb.

A smile appeared among the whiskers.

'Poor old Walter? No one here would touch a bet he made. He's tried, of course, but we're not charity, Sergeant. Jacobson's under the hatches and every bookie knows it.'

'That so? No credit for him, then. A poor man's best off like me, you know, watching a race for the joy of pure athletics. Ah well. Must leave you to your work. Good to see you.'

With a wink and a wave he moved away towards an exit, leaving the pure athletics to continue without his support for the rest of the afternoon and evening.

Harvey had brought in a plateful of roast duck prepared at a restaurant nearby. With the help of the gas-ring it was still warm when Chadwick came into the tent at seven. As soon as he had loosened the champion's boot-laces and cleaned off his face with the sponge, Harvey lifted the plate-cover. He watched for the response to this favourite meal. It was quite five seconds before Chadwick reacted at all, and then it was not the duck that he commented on.

'I am singularly depressed. Open a bottle of wine.'

Harvey lifted a *Graves Supérieur* from the crate behind the clothes-cupboard, drew the cork and poured a small amount into a glass for Chadwick to taste.

'Fill it up, man! This isn't the Café Royal.'

'Sir.'

'And massage my legs, or I'll never get back on the track.'

Harvey applied himself to the task. He knew Chadwick well enough to keep silent at these times. The dinner, which might have been Billy Reid's eel-broth for all the recognition it got, was quickly dispatched.

Chadwick sat back in his chair, moaning abstractedly. At length he addressed the attendant.

'My neck is paining me. See if you can loosen it, will you? I really doubt,' he went on dismally, 'whether I can endure this torment for another three days. The rewards seem less and less worth pursuing as one goes on. And the effort' – he shuddered – 'the effort, Harvey, is almost impossible to muster. It was better on the inside track. Now I'm involved in a physical battle if I try to go any faster than these – these lumbering apes. My ribs ache from the battering they've received. I tell you, this is no race. It's a battle for survival.'

'I've seen, sir,' Harvey agreed. 'They'll put you out if they can. It frets me. But I've listened to their talk. They won't dare knock you down and cripple you. It's the sly nudge and the shin-tap that they use. If they can they'll break your spirit that way. Like,' and he cast about for a comparison that the Captain would appreciate, 'like a siege, sir. Slowly starving you out. Mustn't let morale get low.'

Chadwick reached for an orange.

'I suppose so,' he sighed. 'Tighten my boots, will you? I must get out there again.'

Harvey obeyed, and, as he kneeled, pieces of orange-peel fell about him on the floor.

'You've got to keep on, sir,' he urged. 'For the Regiment, too.'

There was an intensity about Harvey's manner that penetrated even Chadwick's weariness. When he had eaten the orange he swallowed a second glass of wine and stumped back to the track.

Despite the bookmakers' verdict that the interest had been drawn from the race, the stands filled steadily during the evening. Perhaps, as Herriott predicted, the prospect of Chadwick struggling to defend his lead on the outer track was the attraction. Possibly it was interest in Darrell's dramatic death, and the morbid hope of a second collapse. Whatever the reason, the 'gate' amounted to over £400 when it was counted at eleven, almost double the takings for each of the first two days. And the influx greatly enriched the atmosphere in the Hall. For the first time spectators were in the gallery, as well as the stands and the enclosure. The band at its most energetic could not drown the bedlam from around the track, as one favourite or another appeared to gain ground.

The 250-mile landmark – generally reckoned to be the end of the first half of the journey – was reached by several of the entrants during the evening. Chadwick's achievement in reaching this mark as early as two in the afternoon was politely clapped by the handful then present. But when Billy Reid and the Scythebearer hobbled through shortly after ten the roar of acclamation and the waving of hats set the flags above flapping, and flickered the gaslight. The most support came for O'Flaherty. His height and red hair made him an easy figure to pick out, and it was believed that he was the only man left capable of offering Chadwick a serious challenge. Waves of chanting and cheering lifted the Irishman to extraordinary efforts. For almost two hours he was 'mixing' – alternately walking and trotting – making the others' efforts seem puny. Williams, the Half-breed, who had kept pace with O'Flaherty until noon, was forced by blistering to walk on the sides of his boots, and the odds against him doubled between nine and ten. The curiosity of the event, Mostyn-Smith, betrayed no ill-effects from his lack of any sustained sleep since the start. Those who remembered his unenterprising pace on the first day now declared that he had not slowed in the least since then. The dawdler of Monday was going as well as anyone except O'Flaherty and Chadwick.

Herriott stood with Jacobson basking in the sweet din of several thousand voices. A uniformed attendant touched his arm.

'Pardon me, Mr Herriott. Lady at the entrance, asking to speak to you, sir.'

Cora Darrell, now in full mourning, was waiting with her maid-servant. Herriott guided them into an office at the entrance.

'I need hardly say—' began Herriott.

She cut him short.

'Yes. The shock has been very hard to bear. I am afraid I said things yesterday that I now regret. You understand I didn't know the full circumstances. I was not myself.'

114

'Of course,' he conceded. 'You were exceedingly distressed. I could see that. The incident is quite forgiven, quite forgotten. And now tell me how I can assist you.'

'I came to collect Charles's personal things,' Cora explained. 'The detective said that I should come late to avoid the newspaper people. I want to go out to the tent without attracting public attention. Would you escort me, Sol?'

'I shall be most honoured. Is there much to collect? Could I bring the things here for you?'

'No. I want to go myself. Taylor shall carry the suitcase for me. I have a cab calling again in an hour to convey us back to the house.' She paused, hesitating over a question. 'Is Sam Monk still in the building? I cannot face him.'

He touched her forearm reassuringly.

'You shall not see the man, Cora. He has not been allowed near the tent since . . . I saw him early this evening, drinking liquor heavily. He is probably quite inebriated by now. Shall we go at once? This is a time when we will not be noticed.'

They were able to pass easily and discreetly through the crowd, who were moving homewards and unlikely to connect a veiled widow with the mirthful entertainment they had just left. In one respect, however, Herriott had miscalculated. As they turned into the passageway between two stands, leading to the tracks, Sam Monk faced them. He was reaching for support from the side of the stand, and miscalculating the distance. His other hand gripped a half-empty bottle and the contents slopped each time he moved. Although he stood across the passage a yard or two from them, his eyes were held fish-like, unable to vary their focus. Cora automatically stopped short, and drew back behind Herriott's ample form.

Fortunately there was no confrontation. Behind Monk, silhouetted in the square of light at the arena entrance, appeared Walter Jacobson. Finding himself alone in the centre, he was making a strategic move to more obscure regions of the Hall. The snap of Herriott's fingers halted him.

'Walter! Good fellow. Get this man into his hut, will you? He has to stay here. Police orders. I gave him the end hut, farthest from the others being used. Can you manage? Good.'

Cursing himself for choosing that exit at that moment, Jacobson took a firm grip on Monk's jacket collar, and led him, unprotesting, towards the Liverpool Road end. Herriott apologized to Cora, and they moved on, into the arena. Cora's entrance, shrinking between her maid, Taylor, and Herriott, was so unrelated to her arrival in the stadium two days ago that if the band had broken into a fanfare she could have moved on unrecognized. As it was, the little group stepped across the tracks and up to the constable at the tent. After a word of explanation Cora and Taylor were admitted and the lamp inside was ignited for them. Herriott returned to the lap-takers, to settle the next day's roster.

The band were now taking longer rests, wishing away the minutes remaining until midnight, when their stint finished. And in these intervals between light operatic selections and waltzes (marches had been abandoned

116

at the manager's request when the pace of the baton outstripped the competitors) the shouts from the crowd began to echo with increasing resonance. The Hall was emptying steadily. The walkers themselves kept moving, but without the same impetus. Young Reid, who had been much encouraged by reaching the 'halfway mark', drew level with Williams, now wincing with each step. His attempt to open a conversation was repudiated with an obscenity, so he stepped out towards Chalk, who was in better shape.

'Good crowd tonight, wasn't they?'

Chalk nodded. 'You'll find that, young'un. If you can keep on your feet through the first three days, the crowd carries you 'ome.'

'You think they'll still come?'

'Oh yes. Long as we give 'em a show. Always get a lot of 'em at the end of a mix. Like 'errings in a barrel on the last day. You'll see, if you've got any legs left.'

'There's a lot dropped out,' agreed Reid. 'Felt like it myself till tonight. Half the huts is empty now, you know.'

'I've seen. It's time they let us 'ave one to ourselves. I've 'ad my fill of sharing. Got one of those bloody tykes with me. Don't say much, and when 'e do I can't make out a bloody word. Found 'im 'aving a nip of my grog last night. I could've bloody felled 'im if I'd been feeling right.'

'You think we might get a chance of a hut each?' asked Reid, suddenly seeing a prospect of relief from his own room-mate's cynicism.

'If they didn't 'and 'em out to bloody trainers, we might. You see bloody Monk in the end one? Poisons Darrell and

117

they give 'im a hut to 'imself for it. Should be sleeping in the gutter, a bastard like that.'

'You think he meant to do Darrell in?'

'Don't bloody matter. Either way the man's a bastard. If you can't trust a bloody trainer to mix a drink he ought to be made to take a powder 'imself. Sam Monk!' He spat, to punctuate the name. 'If that bugger ever wants another job 'e'd better go round the stables. No ped in London's going to 'ire a gimcrack bastard that killed one of the best pathmen to put on a shoe.'

After that moving eulogy to their dead colleague both men continued in silence until the lights were lowered and they could return to their shared sleeping berths.

THE PEDESTRIAN CONTEST AT ISLINGTON

Positions at the end of the Third Day

Name	Miles	Laps
CAPT. ERSKINE CHADWICK	296	3
FEARGUS O'FLAHERTY	288	0
GEORGE WILLIAMS	263	5
PETER CHALK	261	3
WILLIAM REID	261	0
JAMES GAFFNEY	259	3
DAVID STEVENS	259	0
MONTAGUE LAWTON	258	3
FRANCIS MOSTYN-SMITH	257	4

M. Jenkins (200 miles), W. Holland (192 miles) and C. Jones (188 miles) retired from the race.

10

Thursday

Feargus O'Flaherty slept serenely, his russet curls pressed against the sacking which served as a pillow. The hard work that he had put in the evening before had left him exhausted, but exhilarated. Only eight miles separated him from Chadwick. Eight miles that he could cut back slowly, day by day. With the crowd all behind him, lifting him, he would be level with Chadwick by Saturday, and there would be a great struggle for victory, which he would surely win in the last second. And then how life would alter! His days as a supporting runner, a catchpenny performer included to divert the crowds with his antics, would end. He would be a celebrity, entitled to be matched in duels with the champions. O'Flaherty of Ireland, the Dublin Stag, conqueror of Chadwick in the Six-Day Contest! He would travel to Europe, and America and take on the best of the Indians. And while he was touring abroad, Moira should ride along Regent Street in a phaeton and stop to buy gowns and bonnets wherever she wanted, ready to charm him when he returned . . .

'You will pardon me, O'Flaherty?'

The dreamer stirred, disturbed by the voice.

'I think you should be rousing yourself, my friend. The race, you know. I have just left the track. Chadwick's light is on . . .'

O'Flaherty parted his eyelids. Mostyn-Smith was sitting near by, still in his black outfit, eating a breakfast prepared from some herbal recipe. Harshly this unromantic scene displaced the one in O'Flaherty's mind.

He stretched, tugged the blankets away and rose, yawning.

'I don't know how you stay on your feet on half an hour's rest,' he said to Mostyn-Smith, half in admiration, half resentment.

'If you think it out mathematically,' came the answer, between spoonfuls, 'you will realize that my half-hour is in fact only one hour less than your three. I rest, you see, for four half-hours in twenty-four, whereas you take a single rest-period of three hours, except when your natural functions otherwise compel you to stop.'

The logic of this was too sophisticated for the Irishman in his present state. He moved to the door, dimly recalling that the washing facilities were behind the huts. Mostyn-Smith raised a restraining hand.

'Footwear, O'Flaherty. You should not walk barefoot in those fetid pools outside. I admit to being mistaken about poor Darrell's demise, but the danger of tetanus remains.'

O'Flaherty returned without a word for his socks and

121

boots. The experience of sharing with Double-barrel had not turned out as he once expected, with the little man jumping at the sound of his voice. O'Flaherty's prestige would not easily recover from the incident of the carbolic. When his feet were safely shod, he ventured, shivering, outside.

The washing arrangements for the eight pedestrians still in residence at the huts consisted of four buckets and a tap, at knee-height. Two additional buckets were kept behind a wood-and-sacking construction.

O'Flaherty turned the tap to fill a bucket. The water was icy. He carried his bucket some yards from the tap, to escape the odour from nearby. He cupped his hands, and lifted some water to his face, leaning over the bucket with legs astride to avoid the drops that fell. The contact was chilling, but revived him too. It was the first wash he had given himself in twenty-four hours. Such refinements as footbaths and shaves were impossible without an attendant to heat the water. He straightened, shaking the water from his eyes. Then he breathed in, deeply.

There was a familiar, unpleasant smell in the air that had nothing to do with the stench from the latrines.

O'Flaherty coughed to empty his lungs. He inhaled again, speculatively. He was certain now. Gas. But where was its source? He looked around him. He could see only water-piping. Then he wheeled round, and decided what had happened. The huts themselves had been fitted with gas for lighting and cooking. The escape was from the hut behind him, one of those left empty when runners had

122

retired from the competition. The smell was penetrating the wooden sides.

There was no time to investigate; Chadwick might be on the track already, adding to his lead. O'Flaherty walked back to his hut.

Mostyn-Smith was already asleep. Like some weird fakir he seemed to go into and out of unconsciousness at will. He was a queer cove all right. O'Flaherty felt as uncomfortable when he was like this as when he was conscious. Without sitting, he bolted some ripe cheese and bread, swigged at a bottle which he had now taken to hiding among his spare boots, and left for the track.

It was not as late as he feared. Chadwick was still in the tent being fussed over by his trainer. Only Billy Reid was in action so far; his brother usually made sure he was the first. From behind O'Flaherty came the voices of other competitors returning without enthusiasm, donkeys to the treadmill. Several officials were in the centre, commiserating with each other over their inhuman hours of duty. To their left, Jacobson stood alone. The early start was equally repellent to him, but as manager he could hardly join the complainers. So he stood alone with hands deep in his overcoat pockets, collar turned up to hide unshaven jowls, and legs flexing to combat the draughts. O'Flaherty approached him.

'There's an unholy smell of gas coming from one of the huts. Someone left a tap on, I should say.'

Jacobson responded without much interest. 'Where?'

'The end one. In front of the wash-place. Smelt it when I was there a few moments back.'

'Very well. I'll take a walk that way in a moment.'

O'Flaherty nodded and returned to the track. Chadwick had still not appeared, so he set off at a jog-trot. At this rate he might cut back the eight miles by Friday.

Jacobson consulted his watch, and nodded to Chadwick as he made his appearance. Then he strolled away towards the hut the Irishman had indicated. Only when he was a few yards away did his lethargic thought processes seize on the significance of that particular hovel. He hurried towards the closed door. The whiff of gas was strong around it. The door was stiff, and he used his shoulder. As it swung inwards, an outrush of gas hit his face as firmly as a baize drape. He drew back for air, gulped, and stumbled inside.

Sam Monk's body lay where Jacobson had last seen it, inert on the bed. The gas-ring and the lamp were hissing into the darkness. He silenced them and quit the place, hungry for air. The glimpse he had taken of Monk's appearance told him it would be futile to try to revive him.

His mind seething with half-realized conclusions, Jacobson ran to the constable seated outside Darrell's tent, and alerted him. The Law took over.

'You say O'Flaherty first noticed the gas?'

Sergeant Cribb questioned Jacobson as they approached the hut containing Monk's body.

'Yes. That was a few minutes after four.'

'And you opened up?'

'I did. The gas reeked all round the hut. You can still smell it, can't you?'

Cribb sniffed, and grimaced.

'You had to force the door?'

'Well, it was stiff. I put my shoulder to it.'

They stepped inside. The sergeant bent over the body to examine it. Jacobson swung the door back and forth, encouraging a draught. When it was safe, he lit the lamp.

'There's something written here,' he said, taking up a sheet of paper from the top of the bedside cupboard. He handed it to Cribb, who replaced it on the cupboard without glancing at it.

'Whisky,' he said, finally standing up.

'Oh yes,' Jacobson confirmed. 'The man had been imbibing heavily. I brought him back here about half past ten last night. He was drunk all right.'

The sergeant was interested.

'You brought him, Mr Jacobson?'

'Well, yes.' The manager hesitated. 'Mr Herriott asked me to. Monk was getting in the way. There was a lady. Mrs Darrell. I think Mr Herriott wanted Monk where he could cause her no embarrassment.'

'So you brought him here?'

'Yes. He was far gone, Sergeant. You can see that by his features now. The drink had left him rosy-faced.'

Cribb shook his head.

'Symptom of gassing. Was he conscious, would you say?'

'I suppose so. He was depressed, though. When I brought him in he just sank back on to the bed.'

'Did you turn on the gas?' Cribb was examining the piece of paper as he spoke.

'No. I'm sure of that. I simply brought him in, watched him fall on to the bed and left.'

Cribb grunted, apparently accepting the statement. His eye picked out the ventilator, a small outlet which worked by a shutter mechanism. It was closed.

'Pretty little suicide, eh?' he said to Jacobson. 'Gas soon fills a poky shack like this. Much cleaner than a wrist-slashing. This note ...'

'Yes?' Jacobson was feeling relieved that there was a note. Events might have been interpreted to his disfavour otherwise.

'You've read it?'

Jacobson shook his head, and Cribb obliged by reading it aloud, in the dull intonation traditionally used by police in giving evidence.

'"This is to show how sorry I am. I did not mean him to die. Samuel Monk".'

'His conscience killed him, then,' commented Jacobson. 'Poor fellow. I don't know whether I myself could have carried on living after making the tragic mistake that he did.'

Cribb ignored this. He began feeling into the dead man's pockets.

'The note wasn't here when you brought him in?'

'Certainly not.' Jacobson was puzzled.

'You think it was written after that?'

'Well, I assume it must have been.'

'Capable of writing, was he?' Cribb snapped at him.

Jacobson pursed his mouth irritably.

'You've got the note there, Sergeant, so he must have been. I presume you will identify it as Monk's handwriting.'

'You see the shutter there,' Cribb continued. 'Closed. Was it closed when you were here?'

126

'I really cannot remember,' protested the manager. 'But if a man wanted to gas himself he would hardly leave a ventilator open, now would he?'

Cribb was too taken up with the details of Monk's death to crush this sarcasm. He said nothing more to Jacobson for a full minute.

'Am I wanted any longer?'

'Thank you. No.'

When Jacobson left, Cribb was on his knees, feeling the floor below the bed.

The news was not long in circulating. Cribb's sudden arrival was noted, and Jacobson's agitated comings and goings confirmed an occurrence of some importance. Far from concentrating on their event with the single-mindedness legendary among athletes, the Islington trampers followed every movement within their range of vision. Tedium was a worse menace than distraction in this form of competition. So when a stretcher was carried from the huts past the track the identity of the covered burden was generally known.

'Monk done the proper thing,' was Chalk's verdict. 'If a trainer tips bloody poison into a man's drink 'e's got no right to go on.'

'Bugger 'ad a better ending than Charlie Darrell, come to that,' Williams added. His rest had helped his feet considerably, and he was walking normally now. 'Poor old Charlie. Why bloody Chadwick didn't get it I don't know. That nob's set to take the bloody monkey now, and 'e never had the beatin' of Darrell.'

127

'O'Flaherty's 'ot after him. There ain't ten miles in it and Feargus is no small beer when there's something to go for,' Chalk observed hopefully.

'Beat Chadwick? The day O'Flaherty does that I'll swim the bloody Channel.'

Chalk did not pursue the point. He was not quick-witted at his best, but even he could detect some professional jealousy here. Fortunately a fresh arrival provided distraction.

''Ullo. Crushers arriving in force now,' he commented, watching Thackeray's advance on the hut, where Cribb was still at work. 'I'll tell you something about that one, mate. Master of disguise, 'e is. See them great feet of 'is and that belly? You wouldn't credit that 'e's been running on this path now would you? Double-barrel reckons 'e goes round with him at night—'

A guffaw from Williams broke in.

'You believe that? I'm pussy-footing it with Double-barrel? What's 'e supposed to be up to, for God's sake? That's the only thing we ain't got chasing round this bloody ring – a bobby on 'is beat!' He continued to enjoy the prospect so heartily that Chalk gave up entirely.

Inside the hut where Monk's body was found, Cribb was grappling with blankets on the floor when Thackeray arrived.

'Come on, man. Help me get this lot back on the bed,' he said, a little breathlessly. 'Had to have 'em off. Checking. Heard about Monk?'

'I came as quick as I could, Sarge. Looks as if this ties it all up neat. Sad business, though.'

The two detectives between them deposited the blankets, and then themselves, on the bed.

'Out of condition, both of us,' declared Cribb. 'Could do with a turn or two round the track.' Abruptly becoming serious, he added, 'You saw Monk yesterday, after I left you. What was he like?'

'Like?' queried Thackeray.

'His state. Drinking then, wasn't he?'

'Oh yes. He'd taken a glass or two, but he talked well enough, Sarge.'

'Depressed?'

'I didn't think so at the time, but I'm not really a judge of such things. My wife always—'

'You asked to search his place?'

'Yes. He gave me a key at once. Said there wouldn't be anyone else there. He also told me where to find the phial of strychnine, and it was there, exactly where he said.'

Thackeray produced the tube of glass from his pocket. Cribb took it carefully, held it in front of his face, and turned it slowly, watching the repositioning of the few crystals inside as though it was a water-snowstorm in a glass globe.

'There they are then. He spoke truth,' said Cribb.

'I went on to the chemist he spoke of,' continued the constable. 'The man knew him by name. He remembered supplying the strychnine last Friday too. Said he does a bit of business with the trainers from around here. He knows they use the strychnine for making up tonics for the pedestrians, but, as he says, he's only supplying very small amounts, and he's careful about telling them of its dangers. They all sign the book—'

'Book? Monk had signed for it?'

Thackeray nodded.

'Take a look at this, then.' Cribb picked up the note that Jacobson had found. 'Same signature?'

Thackeray squinted at it, scratching his beard.

'Positively the same, Sarge.'

'Hm.' Cribb seemed suddenly elated. 'Did you look through the book?'

Thackeray beamed virtuously.

'I found seven previous entries in Monk's name in the last four years. They was all for the same quantity, Sarge.'

'Capital work. He was a regular customer, then?'

'Yes – and each time he collected the strychnine he was preparing a ped for a long walk or mix. The chemist told me he made sure of that.'

'Did he now?'

'And I questioned him about other sources of supply,' continued the constable, stressing his efficiency, 'and he told me he didn't know of another chemist his side of London who would sell a man strychnine, unless he was a doctor.'

Cribb was in good humour now. He had quite recovered from being brought out so early.

'Excellent, Thackeray! We're making progress.'

The constable glowed.

'Now! On your knees, man,' Cribb continued. Thackeray's mouth dipped at the sides, to underline exactly the shape of his moustache. 'Look for a pencil. I've had no luck. Man like you should find it if it's here.'

'I've got one in my pocket,' Thackeray replied, much deflated. 'You can borrow that.'

The sergeant slowly shook his head.

'Not your pencil, Thackeray, and not mine. I want Monk's. Else what did he write this note with? There was none in his pockets, and I've been through everything else here.'

Slightly mollified, Thackeray stooped to search for the piece of evidence. Three unsuccessful minutes later he looked up again at Cribb.

'Sarge, it ain't here, I'm sure. You know, it could be that he wrote the note some time earlier. Wasn't he drunk, anyway, when Jacobson brought him back here?'

'True,' said Cribb. 'Staggering drunk. I had to confirm there's no pencil here though. Means he wrote the letter some hours previous. Jacobson brings him in, too scuppered to stand straight, and dumps him on the bed. Some time after Jacobson's left, he gets up, produces this note from somewhere, and puts it out on the cupboard. Then he shuts the air-vent, turns on the lamp and the gas-ring and gets back on the bed. D'you see it happening, Thackeray?'

The constable got to his feet.

'Well, a man can come round quite quick, Sarge. He did that night we questioned him. He wasn't found until after four. That's five hours since Jacobson dumped him.'

'All right. So it's not impossible, even if we think it unlikely. Let's assume that's the way he did it. Now tell me why.'

'Why, Sarge? Well, it's in the note, ain't it? He was so depressed after killing Darrell he took his own life.'

'So you think Monk killed Darrell?'

Thackeray rubbed his forehead. Either the sergeant was being impossibly naive, or too subtle for him to follow.

'Think back to yesterday morning, when we questioned Monk,' explained Cribb. 'If the man killed Darrell accidentally, then he was lying to us. He swore that he put no more strychnine into that bottle than would have helped revive a tired man. You checked the phial and it contains the number of crystals he said it would. The rest, as he told us, had gone into the tonic. Yet somehow the tonic gets a monstrous helping of strychnine – much more than Monk collected from the chemist this time, or in four years together. Now then,' and Cribb's voice was raised in enthusiasm, 'if Monk added more strychnine it wasn't an accident. It was murder, Thackeray.'

'But the note,' protested Thackeray. He picked it up. '"This is to show how sorry I am. I did not mean him to die" – and that's in Monk's own hand.'

Cribb rubbed his hands vigorously.

'Exactly! We've got a case, man – double murder very likely. Don't look depressed. Murder and suicide at the very worst.'

11

Harvey stood alone by the tent, studying the progress of the race. Chadwick had been mistaken in agreeing to make his way with the others on the outer track; he was sure of that. These were toughened professionals; they had clawed through a jungle in which genuine races were unknown, real talent trampled down and every performer the prey of touts and betting gangs. For them, if they survived and developed the necessary cunning, it brought a living; more than they could expect. They were not athletes, any more than street-bears were entertainers. A pedestrian of Chadwick's ability could defeat any of them by fifty miles in fair conditions. But his experience was totally different: he had run only in two-man races since he began as a professional. Before that he had competed as a gentleman amateur in military sports, watching the non-commissioned ranks scrap for pewter, and then outshining their efforts in the officers' race. Good for personal morale, but poor preparation for the outer track at Islington.

They had taken protective measures. Chadwick's shins had been badly bruised, and cut in places. Now they were well-padded under his stockings. It was difficult to do much for his ribs, which had taken a buffeting, but he had learned to adapt his arm-action to protect them. And little could be done about the baulking each time he tried to overtake one of the others. Three or four times they had almost forced him into the crowd. Of course, the mob applauded all this; it was not often that one of the upper classes was exposed to public ridicule.

And that confounded Irishman was getting through each time, picking up a few yards every lap. He seemed not to tire, or blister, and he took only the shortest rests.

Of one thing Harvey was certain: it was the last race that Chadwick would run. Each time the Captain returned to his tent he was more defeated in spirit. The zest for sheer physical mobility, the joy of clipping along the Bath Road through a summer night, had been killed absolutely. Chadwick would take his money and retire. They had been fine times for both of them: Harvey mounted, with sponge, vinegar and a change of clothes, and the Captain out there ahead, conquering the mile-posts.

This race was to blame for everything. It had been cursed from the start. Two men had died. Another, finer man, was being broken. And all around was squalor, squalid people, squalid sounds, squalid smells.

Harvey turned away from the track, and went into the tent.

Early that afternoon a message arrived for Cribb asking him to attend urgently at Islington Mortuary. A doctor was waiting there for him.

134

'The body of a man was brought here early this morning from the Agricultural Hall, Sergeant. I believe that you are in charge of the investigation.'

'Already there on another case, Doctor. This death appears to be connected with the death of Charles Darrell, a professional runner. I shall investigate both, unless I'm otherwise ordered.'

'There is a matter that you should know, then, relating to the body of Samuel Monk. I have not yet made a full examination, but what I discovered is sufficiently important, I think, for you to be informed at once. The head, Sergeant, bears the sign of a blow inflicted before death, but not long before. I think you should see this for yourself.'

Cribb was ushered into the chill room where the body lay, stripped of clothing, on a bench, attended by a mortuary official, well wrapped in an ulster and scarf.

'The hair appears to have been arranged to cover the wound,' explained the doctor, 'but, as you can observe here, there is blood and considerable discoloration. I would estimate that a blow of such force, here below the crown, would render a man senseless.'

'Could he have fallen?' asked Cribb. 'We know he was drunk.'

'I think not. There are no secondary bruises on other areas of the body. By the shape of the wound I would suggest that the poor fellow was struck from behind with a bar-shaped implement, somewhat thicker than a poker.'

'And died soon after, of gas-poisoning,' added Cribb.

'That I shall confirm when I have made a full

examination, Sergeant. The wound seemed to suggest foul play, and I thought it correct to inform you at the earliest opportunity.'

'I'm deeply obliged.'

Cribb replaced his hat, and hurried out to hail a cab.

At the Islington Green end of the Hall, farthest from the row of huts, it was possible to pass through to a minor hall, about a hundred feet square. When the main building was used for its appointed purpose the smaller hall was where the pigs were exhibited. For very pungent reasons it was seldom hired for other functions. Midway through this afternoon, however, a move was made in that direction by the Press representatives. Sol Herriott had agreed to meet them to make a statement, and answer questions.

This meeting was staged with some formality. Chairs and a table had been set out in the centre of the hall, and it was not long before the thirty seats were taken. Expectation buzzed about the gathering, but there was silence when Herriott and Jacobson walked in, and took their positions at the table.

'I shall not keep you long, gentlemen,' Herriott began, hitching his thumbs into his waistcoat pockets, 'for I am as sensitive to atmospheres as you.'

He ventured a laugh, which was not taken up. The Press were there for a statement, not amusement.

'I am here with Mr Jacobson, the manager of this event, to make an announcement of some importance. You will have heard no doubt – indeed, you will have reported in your newspapers by now – that a trainer, Mr Sam Monk,

136

the attendant of the late Mr Darrell was himself found dead in one of the huts early this morning. He died of the effects of gas. A note was found in the hut suggesting that he had taken his own life.

'These tragedies, gentlemen – one following so swiftly on the other – have shocked and saddened us all. Jacobson and I have given much thought to the future of the race, in the light of these misfortunes. We are not insensitive to the suggestions which have been made, not least by some of yourselves, that the race should now be called off, out of respect to the so recently deceased.

'But we have another obligation which we are bound to consider, gentlemen. That is our obligation to the living – to the nine plucky travellers who are at the moment more than halfway through the journey that they commenced last Monday morning. We had to decide whether we could bring ourselves to tell these gallant sportsmen that their efforts were to be terminated, and the race cancelled. I ask you now, gentlemen. Would Charles Darrell or Sam Monk have asked for the race to be terminated? I think not. I think they would wish to see a conclusion. And that is the reason why I now announce that the Six-Day Race will continue as planned. But out of respect to their two colleagues the remaining competitors will be asked to wear black armbands. That is all I have to say at this time, but possibly you have some questions for us?'

The response was immediate.

'Is it not a fact, Mr Herriott,' asked a reporter who had not been seen in the Hall before that afternoon, 'that you

137

are persisting with your promotion at the command of the detective police, so that they may investigate certain irregularities in the two deaths?'

Herriott instantly disliked the man.

'I do not know your name, sir—'

'Pincher, of the *New Examiner*.'

'Thank you, Mr Pincher. The answer to your question is that the police have agreed to let the race to go on. They have certain routine investigations to complete, and it will be convenient for them to conduct these here as the race continues.'

Pincher was still on his feet.

'You say "routine investigations." Do you deny absolutely the rumour at present circulating that Mr Darrell's death was not an accident, but manslaughter, or even murder?'

'That is for the police to decide, sir. Does any other gentleman have a question?'

'Yes.' A reporter in the front row spoke. 'Is it true that Mr Monk steadfastly denied being responsible for Charles Darrell's death?'

'I believe that is so.' Herriott did not like the drift of the questions.

'Then do you have the right to ask the pedestrians in your promotion to honour the memory of a man who now appears to have lied about the death of one of their colleagues?'

It was a difficult point. But Herriott was at his best.

'Gentlemen, we are not detectives. We are not competent to judge Mr Monk. If negligence is proved, that may alter our opinion. But until that is the case, I shall respect his memory as I respect Mr Darrell's. Our system of justice is founded on similar principles. Shall we now confine our discussion to the world of the living? Are there any inquiries from you about the progress of the race, which, I need hardly remind you, is now entering a most interesting phase?'

The Press were not so easily deflected. Pincher stood up again.

'Since you do not propose to discuss the two deaths that have occurred during your promotion, perhaps you will say something about your arrangements for the' – he paused – 'safety and health of the participants.'

Herriott did not recognize the trap.

'Certainly—'

'In that case,' snapped Pincher, 'would you explain how the two doctors who are allegedly in attendance during this event failed to recognize the symptoms of strychnine poisoning when Charles Darrell collapsed?'

It was a neat manoeuvre. Herriott did not disguise his annoyance.

'Gentlemen. Mr Darrell's collapse was fully discussed when you questioned me yesterday. If some of you were not then present' (he glared at Pincher) 'I do not regard it as my duty to apprise you now of matters which were disposed of then. Is there another question, please?'

Clearly, Herriott would not be drawn.

'I have a question for Mr Jacobson.' The speaker was another newcomer.

Herriott turned towards the manager, hoping he was equal to the inquisition. Jacobson got to his feet.

'I believe, sir,' said the reporter, 'that you were the last to see Mr Monk alive.'

'That is true.'

'It would be interesting to know whether he made any confession of negligence in the matter of Mr Darrell's death.'

'He made none, sir, beyond what was written in the note.'

'Ah yes. Is it true, Mr Jacobson, that the trainer was – not to mince words – in a drunken state when you left him?'

'He had been drinking, I think, yes.'

There was laughter.

'We have it on good evidence, sir, that you were holding him up.'

Jacobson nodded uncomfortably.

'I provided some support.'

Herriott was on his feet, and shouting. 'I refuse to allow this cross-examination to continue. If you want it in plain words, Monk was blind to the world, and Jacobson got him to bed. He was found in the morning, five hours later, when gas was smelt by one of the competitors. That is all that we have to say on this matter.'

At once a dozen of the audience hurried from the Hall. Fleet Street's crime division had got its statement on the Islington Deaths Mystery, and the genuine sporting correspondents were left to extract what they could for their columns. By stages, Herriott became less hostile, and answered questions on the daily attendances, the status of Chadwick, and the plans for the victory cere-mony. Only when a question was put to him about the cramped accommodation did another outburst threaten. Fortunately, Jacobson tugged at Herriott's arm, and after a short consultation, the promoter announced:

'This is a matter which has been our concern since the commencement of the race. Happily I can now disclose that we shall be able this evening to re-allocate the vacated huts. It will no longer be necessary for the competitors to share accommodation.'

Feeling this was a positive achievement, Herriott closed the meeting.

'One of these, I shouldn't wonder.'

Sergeant Cribb was standing with Thackeray by the huts, which were unoccupied. The tenants were all away at the track. A large afternoon audience was in the Hall, making itself heard above the band's blare. The competitors were out there, entertaining them.

Cribb had picked up one of a pile of iron struts of various lengths, that had been used in the construction of the hut roofs. This one was about eighteen inches long, and the thickness of a walking-cane. It could make an ugly weapon.

'Heavy enough to do the job, and the right size. One good swing at the back of his skull when he's lying there, turned over towards the wall. Child could have done it with a bar like this.' He swung it sharply through the air, bringing it down hard into his other palm. 'I bungled, Thackeray. Should have looked closer for signs of foul play.'

'It seems to me,' Thackeray consoled him, 'that as

141

the party that bashed him pulled the hair neat over the wound you couldn't be expected to find it, Sarge.'

'Hm. Should've checked. Whole thing was too neat. Still, that's past. Lesson to us both. Point is, Thackeray, the man was bashed and left to die.'

'To make it seem he took his own life.'

'Yes. With a note in his own handwriting beside him. How that was done bothers me. I'm having it looked at, compared with other writings from his hand. He could have planned on suicide anyway, of course. I don't think so, though. No, Mr Monk knew he was clear the moment we suggested checking his lodging. And men of his sort don't take to suicide unless the hangman threatens.'

'So we're left with two murders,' commented Thackeray.

Cribb tossed down the bar and brought his hands up to grip the constable's arm.

'That's the sum of it, Thackeray. Name your suspects.'

Thackeray looked about him cautiously. The din behind them continued. Everyone else was absorbed in the race.

'It's hard to know which to start with. I suppose Jacobson's the prime suspect. He's deep under the hatches, you found out, and he was the last to see Monk alive. He could have fixed a heavy bet somewhere on Chadwick, and downed Darrell to settle his debts. Then he'd fake the suicide to put the rap on Monk.'

'Good. We'll watch him. Who else?'

'Chadwick himself. He stands to make a mint of money out of this, and Darrell was his only rival – but going too well that first day. It wouldn't do for a nob like Chadwick to get beat by one of Darrell's class.'

142

'Motive – honour of the regiment. Right. Any other nominations?'

'I've got a queer fancy about Herriott, Sarge. Suppose he backed Chadwick to win so that his bets would cover any loss on the promotion. Darrell's form on that first day might have panicked Herriott into trying to nobble him. He could have tipped in more strychnine than he realized. A purler or two among the runners is good business, too. Listen to that crowd.'

'Sol Herriott, then. You're doing famously. Who else?'

Thackeray was encouraged. He expanded on his theories, shaping the whiskers under his chin to a point as he spoke.

'Ah. Outsiders, mostly. Who stands to gain most? O'Flaherty, I reckon; Chadwick, of course; maybe Chadwick's trainer. I don't know his name, but I've seen the man around. He keeps to himself.'

'Harvey.'

'Him, then. And this doctor bloke – Mostyn-Smith. I can't make out what he's doing in this affair. I suppose, if you look at it logical, anyone here after ten-thirty last night could have fixed Monk. Then we've got to find which of them had a motive for killing Darrell. Perhaps we ought to know more about him, Sarge.'

'First-rate suggestion,' declared Cribb. He was beginning to form an affectionate respect for Thackeray's painstaking deductions. 'We'll go and see the one suspect you missed. Should tell us more about Darrell, and might clear up a few mysteries about herself.'

'Herself?'

'Mrs Darrell, Constable. Never discount the lady.'

'But I don't see how—'

'She's visited this Hall twice. First time, the afternoon before Darrell went down. Second time, last night.'

12

Mrs Darrell was not at home. The detectives explained to Taylor, who opened the door of the Finsbury Park house no more than the distance between her eyes, that they were aware of the time. It was dusk, and misty at that, and too late to be calling on a lady. But they were officers of the law, and their visit was essential to their enquiries. It could not be postponed. If Taylor would be so kind as to pass this on to her mistress, might she not agree to seeing them? Cribb summoned a winning smile. Thackeray stamped the tiled path and flapped his arms to emphasize the cold. Taylor closed the gap until only one eye was visible. Mrs Darrell was not at home.

Cribb fixed the eye with a look of authority.

'This is police business. Important business. We must see Mrs Darrell tonight. If she's out, I must insist that you tell me where she is and when you expect her to return.'

The response was immediate.

'The Mistress is at Highbury, visiting friends – the Darbys. She always goes there for tea on Thursdays. I expect she'll get back before seven.'

'We'll wait,' announced Cribb. 'Inside, if we may.'

After a moment's hesitation the eye disappeared, and there was the sound of a door-chain being released. Then Taylor admitted them.

'That's better, love,' said Cribb. 'Doesn't do to keep Mr Robert standing on the doorstep, does it? This is Constable Thackeray – good man to have in the house on a lonely November night. You remember me?'

The twitch of her lips showed that she did. She seemed uncertain what to do with her visitors now they had gained entrance.

'We'll not trouble with the drawing-room,' Cribb went on. 'Thackeray here's a burly fellow. Likely as not he'll tumble over the small tables she's got in there. We'll come in the kitchen with you. Smells good to me. What's on the stove?'

Without protesting, Taylor led them through a curtained archway and down some steps to the kitchen. She was a bright-eyed girl in her twenties, without the deportment of a girl of better class. But her figure was so generously proportioned that any movement in the close-cut black dress was attractive to the visitors.

Cribb marched into the kitchen with the air of a prospective purchaser.

'Good,' he said. 'Chance to prove our credentials.' He picked up a bowl from the table-top. 'What d'you make of this, Thackeray?'

The constable saw the point of the game. He sniffed professionally at the bowl.

'Chicken-broth, I'd say, Sarge. Probably made up from Sunday's joint.'

'Good,' said Cribb. 'Followed by . . . '

'An orange, peeled by hand.'

Taylor's eyes gaped wide.

'Not so difficult,' commented Thackeray in a superior tone. 'You threw all the peel on the fire, but look at your finger-nails – right hand.'

'Oh, very smart,' said Taylor without much admiration in her voice. Now tell me what else I had for tea.'

'One large muffin,' answered Thackeray, unperturbed. He lifted a toasting-fork from a patch of crumbs at one end of the table. 'Very fattening that.'

And you finished it all off with a cigarette – ah, now you blush!' declared Cribb. 'Taken from the late Master's rooms, I dare say – or is the Mistress a secret smoker herself?'

'How d'you know that?' Taylor demanded.

'The smoke,' Cribb explained. 'Even the orange can't stop that from lingering. Like me to open a window?'

Giggling at the discovery of her secret, Taylor lit the gas under the kettle. Cribb judged that the time was right for serious questions.

'Your evening off, Monday, you said?'

She turned from the stove.

'That's right,' she said archly, 'I'm courting steady, though.'

'Pretty lass like you would be. Simple deduction that. You were out with your young man last Monday, then?'

'That's right.'

'Quite late, I expect?'

Taylor was blushing. 'Not all that late.'

147

'Back by midnight, then?'

'Before that. Mistress won't have me coming in after.' She filled the teapot, trying to appear uninterested in the questions.

'Mistress have any visitors that evening?'

'Don't know, rightly. She went out to dinner, but didn't bring no one home.' She simpered, concealing something.

'Dinner? Who with?' asked Cribb.

'I'm sure I don't know.'

Self-protection, rather than loyalty, was making her reluctant to talk.

Cribb tried again.

'Could have been one of several, you mean.'

'Well, it weren't her husband,' Taylor said with emphasis.

Cribb pressed her.

'When you came back – before midnight – she was home, then?'

'She was.' The hint of a smile was still there.

'And alone?'

'And alone,' repeated Taylor.

'Hasn't always been like that, eh?' asked Cribb, recalling a confidence Taylor had hinted at before.

'I'm sure I don't know what you mean.'

'Lonely for a ped's wife, when he's in training.'

She caught the ironical note in his voice, and echoed it.

'Oh, terrible lonesome. Poor lady's beside herself with loneliness.'

'Or beside others, eh?' suggested Cribb.

'Now, now, Mister!'

'But nobody on Monday night?'

'I never said that,' Taylor corrected him. 'I said she brought no one home.'

'Someone was already here?'

Taylor threw back her head laughing.

'You a detective? No, Mister, nobody was here, and I saw nobody all night. That didn't stop me hearing a cab draw up in the early morning, and leave two hours later. But don't you let on to Mistress I said that. I'll say it's not true, not a word of it. I could have been dreaming, couldn't I?'

'The early morning? What time?'

'Oh, after one, I'd say. Maybe nearer two.'

'Who opened the door?'

She giggled. 'I didn't, I'm sure of that. She must have – no, I remember. Whoever it was let himself in. I heard a key turn in the latch.'

'Heard no voices?'

'I wouldn't have, unless they was shouting, and they didn't do that. D'you take sugar?'

It was clear that Taylor had said all that she would about the early morning visitor. Cribb returned to small-talk and tea.

A few minutes after this one of the set of signal-bells above the door jerked into life.

'Front door,' announced Taylor, on her feet at once. 'Mistress, I'm sure.' She hurried away to answer the summons. In a minute she returned.

'Mistress will see you in the drawing-room in five minutes.' She lowered her voice, confidentially. 'I'm in a nice pickle for bringing you gents in here.'

Cribb gave his unfailing wink.

'We'll tell her we took you by storm.'

Soon enough formality was restored to the household and Taylor ushered the detectives starchily into Cora's presence. She sat in a shell-backed easy chair. A pair of upright rosewood chairs had been set out for the visitors.

'I am sorry that I was out,' Cora began, 'but if you had made an arrangement I should have made a point of being here.'

Cribb accepted the mild reproof.

'Mrs Darrell, I don't know whether you heard this morning's news.'

'Of what, Sergeant?'

'Oh – er – Monk's death, Ma'am.'

She whitened at once. The ticking of the clock, under a glass dome, suddenly seemed to increase in power, a pulse-beat magnified many times.

'Sam Monk – dead?'

'Died of gas-poisoning, Ma'am.'

Her thoughts struggled for a logical sequence.

'You mean ... dead? Suicide? He took his own life? Blamed himself—'

'Not exactly, Mrs Darrell. We think he was probably murdered.'

Cribb watched her reaction most closely. Her eyelids were lowered as she absorbed this second shock. Her hands tightened their grip on the handkerchief she held until the fingers became drained of blood. When she eventually found words, she was coherent.

'Who would kill him? Why should anyone want to

murder Sam?' An implication of Monk's murder dawned on her. 'You think someone blamed him for Charlie's death, and killed him for it. You can't believe that I . . . He was an old friend, Sergeant. I said some terrible things about him. Perhaps he *was* negligent. I might have sued him – but murder! That isn't a woman's way.'

'That's open to discussion,' Cribb said. 'And I'm not suggesting anything to involve you in this. But let's get the facts right. Evidence seems to exonerate Monk.'

'What do you mean?'

'The tonic, Ma'am. He mixed it perfectly. Just as the recipe said. Someone else must have tipped in the strychnine.'

'I don't understand how—' Cora was dazed.

'Don't you try, Ma'am. That's our job in Detective Department. Ready to answer some questions, are you? We need to know more about your husband. Got to find why someone should want to poison him.'

'I shall try to help.'

'Good. Anyone owe your husband money – unpaid bets, or anything of that sort?'

'I feel sure I should know if there was anyone. Charles has never mentioned such a thing.'

'No grudges – old scores? Top-class runner. He must have pricked a few reputations on the way up.'

'I think he was well liked, Sergeant. He had no enemies that I heard of, and many friends.'

'How did he get along with Chadwick? Did they race together before this?'

'I don't think he knew the man. I believe Mr Chadwick

doesn't usually participate in open contests. I've never spoken to him, and I doubt whether Charles did.'

'So there couldn't have been any pre-race agreements about pace and so on. It's not unusual in footracing, I believe.'

'I think not, although I can't be certain. The trainers may have arranged something, of course.'

'And your husband would run to Monk's orders?'

'Well, no. Sam generally left Charles to manage his own running, but I suppose he might have told him to run a certain pace this time. He was more of an assistant and masseur than an adviser. He was a friend too. I think Charles liked to have his support.'

'You and your husband made many friends through his running?'

'Yes.'

'Some would visit this house socially?'

'Some of them, yes.' A note of caution entered her voice.

'Some came when your husband was away training at Hackney, didn't they?'

Her head automatically jerked towards the door that Taylor had closed.

'Friends of both of you, of course,' Cribb added. He was working hard to keep her confidence buoyant.

'Yes. A few times.'

'Foot-racing people – runners and so on?'

'Yes.'

Time for a difficult question. He got up and added a piece of coal to the sinking fire. When he turned to face her, his voice was soft, but his eyes lynx-like.

'I'm interested in last Monday evening. You'll tell me who came then, won't you, Ma'am?'

The response was instantaneous.

'I was out on Monday evening.'

'Oh yes. Visiting the Hall?'

'No. I dined out – with friends.'

'You won't mind me asking,' said Cribb, in a way that he had of assuming co-operation. 'I have to cover this time carefully. Who were these friends?'

This time she did hesitate before answering.

'The Darbys.'

'People you've just left. See them often, do you?'

'They are old friends.'

'Highbury, you said, Mrs Darrell?'

'Holly House, in Gittins Lane.'

Cribb glanced towards Thackeray. The information was already being noted. The constable's writing was accurate, but laborious, and it was understood between them that he would record only essential information.

'What time did you get back from Highbury, Ma'am?'

'About twelve, I think. No, it must have been earlier. I was home before Taylor, and she gets in by midnight.'

'And then, Ma'am?'

Her mouth tightened.

'What do you mean?'

'After you got home, Mrs Darrell. You might not see the importance of this, but we have to cover everyone's movements. Did you go to bed?'

'Not at once. I sat in this room.'

There was a difficult pause, while Cribb waited for her

to continue. She said no more. At length he broke the silence.

'I didn't want to put my next question, Ma'am. It's now necessary. But I'll save you some embarrassment by answering it myself. You had a visitor after you got back.'

She did not respond, but looked through Cribb, visually obliterating him.

'I shouldn't press you if this wasn't deuced important,' he explained. 'We're professional men, Mrs Darrell. We are trained to be discreet. I've information that you had a caller after midnight – early Tuesday morning, in fact. Who was that, please?'

Quite suddenly Cora's poise collapsed.

'This isn't fair!'

She bowed, weeping into the handkerchief, her shoulders convulsing with each sob. Her voice rose and fell hysterically.

'How can you keep tormenting me like this? You come here telling me that Charles is dead, and probably mur- dered, and then you suggest that I entertained a man here on the night before he died. Who are you to make these accusations? I want my father here when you question me. It isn't fair! Why should I tolerate this?'

Cribb waited until the sobbing became more con- trolled. He spoke in a low voice, quite slowly.

'You deny that a man came here that night?'

She jerked her face free of her hands. Her eyes, red- dened by the outburst, flashed fury.

'I have *nothing* to answer to this impertinent question. I think that you had better leave this house.' She reached for the bell-rope.

154

'We shall then, Ma'am,' said Cribb, quite calmly. 'But do consider this. Your husband died on Tuesday. His trainer was murdered yesterday. You could be in danger too. If you're keeping information from us it may prevent us stopping this. I'll ask you no more questions, Ma'am. I apologize for upsetting you. If you should think again – or if you need help – you can contact the police office at the Hall. They'll find me at once. Good evening to you.'

Outside, the fog had thickened. By midnight it would be as dense as Sunday's. After trying for a hansom for twenty minutes, they decided to take a bus. Cribb was determined to return to the Hall before signing off for the night.

'I counted nine of the poor perishers still on their feet,' explained the sergeant. 'I want to check that if any *have* dropped out it's not with a knife between the shoulders.'

An empty twenty-six seater halted at the stop. The horses then pulled away at startling speed through the gathering mist.

'She was lying, wasn't she, Sarge?' said Thackeray, when they had staggered to a front seat.

'You think so? That's something you'll be checking for me tomorrow. Get to Highbury real early. I want you to see these Darby people before she does. Put the question carefully. Ask when they last saw her before today. They're probably close friends, so don't let 'em think it's to her disadvantage.'

'Right. I really meant, Sarge, that she was lying about not having a night visitor.'

Cribb clicked his tongue impatiently.

155

'Won't do, Constable. A bobby needs a better ear than that. You *were* listening?'

'Why, yes.'

'Should have noticed she didn't deny it. Simply refused to answer the point.'

Thackeray nodded sheepishly.

'No matter,' said Cribb brightly, seeing that his criticism had been taken hard. 'You think she had a visitor. That's the main thing.'

Thackeray reacted at once.

'Yes, and I fancy I know who it was.'

'How's that then?'

Cribb liked to affect ignorance with Thackeray. It brought out the constable's best qualities, and often encouraged a point worth taking up.

'By deduction, Sarge.'

The back of Thackeray's left hand, large and shaggy, appeared a foot in front of Cribb's nose. Deduction meant points to Thackeray, and points required fingers.

'Number one: the visitor comes at night between one and two and leaves two hours later. That looks heavy odds on someone from the race. Someone who had to leave when the runners took to bed and be back before they was off again.'

'Good.'

'Two: that don't sound like a runner to me. Poor coves were too beat even on that first day to spend their rest hours visiting women. So it wouldn't have been Darrell himself. Three: it must have been a trainer or a time-keeper. Everyone else could have taken other times

156

off. Four: the timekeepers are too old for that kind of caper.'

'You're doing famously,' admitted Cribb. 'But you've only one finger left.'

'Five: the one trainer connected with Cora was Monk. He showed her the tent that afternoon, and likely had fixed the meeting then.' He withdrew the fist triumphantly.

'First-class,' declared Cribb. 'But tell me this. If Cora was sweet on Sam Monk why did she plan to sue? Long time since I saw a woman so roused against a man.'

Thackeray beamed in a superior fashion. Then he tapped his forehead.

'The mind, Sarge. I fancy I knows a bit about the workings of a woman's thoughts. Cora gets bored while Darrell trains, and looks about a bit. Probably takes a lover or two to while away the six weeks. Agrees to let Monk have his way on Monday night. Next day, Darrell drops dead. What's a woman going to feel like? Feelings of guilt, I reckon, Sarge. That's why she turned on Monk.'

'Plausible,' agreed Cribb, who had listened tolerantly.

The driver reined his horses. They were back in Liverpool Road, although it was barely recognizable in the conditions. In the street Cribb took up the conversation again.

'I like your theory. Stands up well. Came to the same conclusion myself. Different route though. Remember when we grilled Monk? He admitted he was with a lady that night. Must have been her.'

Thackeray snapped his fingers at this realization, and the two detectives, confirmed in their conclusion, set their powers of detection to finding the Hall entrance.

157

The contrast was extreme between the muffled trundling of carriage-wheels, ghost-like, in the foggy streets and the brass din of the Hall band. The scene inside was highly animated. Most of the action, however, came from the bandleader and the crowd. The walkers – none of them could be described as anything else and several hardly merited that – moved mechanically around the circuit. The slightest alteration in the pace was at once taken up by sections of the crowd, who, amazingly, seemed entirely pleased with the entertainment. A trainer offering a sponge, or a competitor leaving the track for a few minutes produced gales of jeering and ribald comment. And the protagonists themselves moved on unperturbed, incongruously drab beneath the flags and flickering chandeliers. Chadwick changed his clothes regularly; the others too obviously ate and slept in their 'racing togs', and had not used a razor or comb since they started.

There was noisy support for O'Flaherty, who had continued with his extraordinary effort to overhaul Chadwick. The scoreboard, on which each man's mileage was hung in numbered plates, now showed only four miles' difference between them. Each time O'Flaherty overtook, the man concerned would move to his right, allowing the Dublin Stag to pass inside. Chadwick, of course, did not benefit from this assistance. In a day's walking the ground gained in this way did not amount to much for O'Flaherty, but the annoyance that registered on Chadwick's face from time to time was a great psychological fillip.

For a few minutes Cribb followed the race from the officials' entrance, with Thackeray yawning at his shoulder.

Jacobson passed, and catching Cribb's eye felt bound to speak.

'It's building up to a promising finish.'

'Looks like it – if they make it.'

Jacobson chuckled.

'Oh, they will now. Most of this bunch are old hands. They're saving something for Saturday. They should sleep better tonight, because we've given them a hut each.'

'Hm. Hope none of 'em leave the gas on.'

With a weak grin, Jacobson passed on through the crowd. Cribb addressed Thackeray, without looking away from the tired procession.

'This goes on two more days, that's all. Two days to find our killer. When this breaks up our chances are small.'

'Nil, I'd say, Sarge.'

'Got to narrow it down according to evidence. You know who we want, don't you? Trouble is, fixing it in black and white for a judge and twelve. Tomorrow, Thackeray, I want you to check the Highbury business early. Then get every Force in London alerted. Every footloose copper. You know the routine. I want the poison books checked at each supplier in London. Get the instructions straight. Strychnine sold in any quantity this last six months. Must have a record of the name, date and amount. I need it by Saturday.'

THE PEDESTRIAN CONTEST AT ISLINGTON

Positions at the end of the Fourth Day

Name	Miles	Laps
CAPT. ERSKINE CHADWICK	381	4
FEARGUS O'FLAHERTY	377	3
PETER CHALK	351	3
GEORGE WILLIAMS	349	0
FRANCIS MOSTYN-SMITH	345	2
JAMES GAFFNEY	341	5
MONTAGUE LAWTON	338	1
DAVID STEVENS	337	3
WILLIAM REID	329	0

13

Friday

Francis Mostyn-Smith had decided who the next victim would be. During his solitary circuits in the small hours of Friday he found time to contemplate the crimes. One could not hope to make deductions when the entertainment was at its height, with an ill-disciplined crowd and those lamentable instrumentalists bombarding one's ears. But at night, in an arena deserted by all but one official, concentration was possible.

He had not conclusively identified the murderer. That was more difficult than nominating a victim. He wondered about approaching the police officers with his information. In the morning they would be back in the Hall continuing their investigations. But something made him reluctant to do this. The sergeant in charge of the detective inquiry, the tall, sharp-eyed fellow, did not have the look of a sympathetic listener. His overweight assistant, who had been exhausted after that one lap of the track, might be more approachable, but probably lacked the intelligence to follow the argument. In all the circumstances it was best, Mostyn-Smith decided, to thwart the assassin himself. He would warn the victim.

O'Flaherty was soundly asleep, cooling his feet in Dublin Bay, when Mostyn-Smith entered his hut. When the reallocation of huts had been made at 1 a.m., O'Flaherty had agreed to move to the empty shack next to the one where Monk had been found. It was smaller than the other, but less draughty, and the bed was softer. The smell of carbolic was not so obvious, either. And Doublebarrel had kept the hut at the opposite end of the row; he would have to find someone else to pester.

It was 3.30 a.m. O'Flaherty was not one of those efficient sleepers who wake at precisely the required time. His brain was not attuned to regular sleep, and this may have accounted for it. But in one respect it was totally reliable; if anything should wake him before his chosen time he knew at once that he was being cheated of sleep.

'O'Flaherty,' Mostyn-Smith ventured in a whisper.

No movement.

'O'Flaherty, old fellow!' A voiced greeting, with a tap on the shoulder.

Complete absence of any reaction.

'O'Fla-her-ty!' Four syllables mispronounced loudly six inches from the one visible ear.

The Stag was back from Dublin, and awake, but he refused to give any sign of it. Perhaps the voice would go away.

Jesus! What was that?

Mostyn-Smith had found a damp sponge and was

162

squeezing it over the Irishman's face. He jerked into a sitting position, grabbed Mostyn-Smith by the shoulders of his running-zephyr and yanked him off balance, so that he fell across the bed.

'If you don't bloody leave me alone, you little bugger, I'll strangle you with these hands!'

Murder was exactly the matter Mostyn-Smith had come to discuss. But for the moment he was speechless, and sightless, for his spectacles had been swept off his nose.

'What is it this time?' demanded O'Flaherty. He was an appalling sight, with bloodshot eyes bolting inside a frame of red hair and four days' growth of beard. Fortunately perhaps, Mostyn-Smith was unable to see him. He groped frantically about the blankets for his glasses. The Irishman seriously began to suspect that Double-barrel was drunk. At last the glasses were found and planted on his face.

'I should apologize—' he began.

'So you bloody well should!'

'It is of the profoundest importance, I do assure you. You see, I had to speak with you before anyone else was awake.'

'You made sure of that. What's the bloody time?'

'Oh, it must be approaching a quarter to four. Now please listen to me. I am convinced that your life is in grave danger, O'Flaherty.'

'And what in God's name makes you think that?'

Mostyn-Smith had recovered some of his poise with his glasses.

'It is all a matter of deductive principles,' he explained, but got no further.

163

'Now hear this, Mister,' growled O'Flaherty. 'You've just destroyed a beautiful sleep, and, so help me, I've beaten men senseless for less. You come in here and tell me I'm going to be killed and then you blabber about principles. Father Almighty, if there's killing to be done stay my hand now!'

'I merely wanted—'

'Just tell me, in simple words, why you won't leave me alone.' O'Flaherty's mood was swinging from aggression to desperation. 'I'm in danger, am I? Well, tell me this. Have you seen a looney outside with a bloody sledgehammer looking for me? If you haven't I'm not interested.'

'I'll be brief,' promised Mostyn-Smith. 'Mr Darrell is dead, and Monk is dead. You must be the next.'

'And why, in God's name, should that be?'

'Don't you see? Somebody required Captain Chadwick to win the race. Therefore Darrell has to be stopped. They gave him poison hoping his death would appear to be due to tetanus. And when strychnine was found to be the cause they tried to make it appear that Monk had made a grievous error and then committed suicide. But the post-mortem examination proved that he, too, had been murdered.'

'You said you'd be brief.'

'And so I have. Can't you see that this homicidal ruffian, whoever he is, will not allow anyone to defeat Captain Chadwick? Your splendid efforts on the track have made you a serious contender, a rival to the Captain. You have become an unexpected obstacle to our murderer's plan, and he will try to remove you, be sure of that.'

164

'Thank you,' said O'Flaherty, without much gratitude in the words. 'So I'm next for the strychnine. And I'll tell you something that might surprise you, Double-barrel. It'll be a mercy to feel the spasms coming on because I'll know that in no time at all I'll be free for ever from you and your bloody safety precautions! Now will you get out and leave me fifteen minutes' rest before I go to the slaughter?'

Nodding appeasingly, Mostyn-Smith backed towards the door. the reception had not been exactly what he anticipated, but the Irishman was an irascible fellow, and might ponder the logic of the argument when he had controlled his temper. At least one could now return to one's own endeavours with an unspotted conscience. None the less, he would keep a fatherly eye on the Irishman.

Sergeant Cribb arrived at the Hall early, conscious that there was much to do. Progress had been made, but it would have to be accelerated. Thackeray's inquiries into the supplier of the poison might provide a lead, yet there was precious little time in which to follow it up. A false name was sure to have been used, and descriptions from shopkeepers were generally altogether too vague. The main possibility of progress was still in the Hall itself. All the suspects except Cora Darrell were there, committed to remain in the Hall until 10.30 p.m. on Saturday.

He had examined the case by every orthodox procedure: suspects, means and opportunity, and possible motives. The timing of the crimes, he knew, was fundamental, but it was complicated by the nature of Darrell's death. The act of murder had been committed not when Darrell breathed his last, nor when he first collapsed, but at some time before he drank the 'bracer' at 4 a.m. on Tuesday morning. Monk had made up the potion at his lodgings and brought it to the Hall with the other provisions on Sunday night. Some time in the next twenty-four hours the murderer had got into the tent, found the bottle and added the strychnine. If Monk were eliminated, as he had to be now, the possibility of the murderer adding the poison to the drink while Darrell was in the tent was remote. So it was probably done some time during Monday, when Monk and Darrell were occupied with the race.

Who had reasons for going into the tent? Darrell, Monk, Herriott – as promoter, Jacobson – as manager, Chadwick (possibly) as a fellow-competitor concerned about mutual facilities and Harvey for a similar reason. Cora, he knew from the newspapers, had been in the tent when she visited the Hall on Monday afternoon, but that was with Monk. Could she and Monk have arranged her husband's death between them; and would she later have battered Monk to fake the suicide? It was conceivable, for the trainer was already in a stupor and it would not need a powerful blow from one of those metal struts to see that he remained that way.

So up to five people could have entered the tent without being challenged. And then Cribb remembered. He delved thumb and forefinger into his fob and took out a crumpled piece of newspaper, the account of Monday's

166

events in the Hall. His thumbnail settled below a particular sentence.

The dressing and feeding accommodation of Chadwick and Darrell contains every appliance for their comfort and convenience; your columnist examined the latter's commodious tent and considered it worthy of housing a campaigning monarch on some foreign field of battle.

Cribb winced. The entire sporting Press had to be added to the list of those who could have got into the tent. Abandoning the matter for the moment, he walked over to Chadwick's tent.

'Mr Harvey?'

The trainer looked up from a newspaper. He was having a late breakfast of kidneys refused by the Captain that morning.

'My name's Cribb – Sergeant Cribb. You've probably seen me about the Hall these last few days. You look after Mr Chadwick, don't you?'

'Captain Chadwick.'

'That's right. Point is, I need to interview him. Straighten out some facts, you know. When's he coming off the track?'

Harvey was dubious. 'He comes off at noon, for about twenty minutes, but he won't welcome questions. He needs all the time for his lunch.'

'I understand. Shan't keep him long. I'll be here at twelve, then. Oh, and er – Mr Harvey.'

'Yes?'

'Once you've dished up the tripe and onions, be a stout fellow and leave me alone with the guv'nor, will you? Confidential questions, you know.'

There was resentment in Harvey's nod of acquiescence.

'Fact is, Captain Chadwick, I need your help.'

Cribb was sitting opposite the Champion, who was eating hungrily, avoiding the sergeant's keen gaze.

'I need your help,' Cribb repeated. 'Comes to a point when you've tried every deuced line of inquiry you know, and nothing's come out of it. So I ask myself what's to be done. And the answer comes back: get some help. Now you're a man of education and a military expert too. Strikes me that if anything untoward happened in this arena it wouldn't pass your notice. I'm right, sir, aren't I?'

Chadwick sniffed, and took a mouthful of cold chicken. Cribb's persuasive sallies rarely sank without trace. He was floundering now.

'You'd have noticed the comings and going at Darrell's tent on Monday, for example?'

Another bite at the chicken leg.

Cribb persevered. 'I believe the reporters were shown the living quarters, and later Mrs Darrell came to see the tent.'

Silence again.

At last Captain Chadwick lifted his napkin to his lips and moustache, wiped them and tossed it aside.

'For your information – Sergeant' – and he spoke the rank as though he were addressing a crossing-sweeper – 'I

168

am not in the pay of the constabulary, and I feel myself under no obligation to act as their informant. If you wish me to answer questions, then kindly put them in a civil fashion, and not in these obsequious subterfuges.'

'Very well, sir. How many times have you raced against the late Charles Darrell?'

'None before this event.'

'You had not met him before Monday?'

'We met to sign articles last week. It is the custom in two-man races,' explained Chadwick, 'and ours was a race within a race.'

'Did you have any communication with him before then?'

'Merely through the medium of the newspaper that usually arranges such events. He was not the class of man that I am accustomed to meeting with.'

'And your trainer?' Cribb continued. 'Was he in touch with Darrell or his trainer?'

'I had Darrell watched, if that is what you mean,' answered Chadwick. 'It is customary to study one's adversaries at their training – though I hardly know why, for my own strategy is unalterable.'

'And Mr Harvey gave you reports on Darrell's showing at Hackney?' continued Cribb, ignoring the last remark. 'Were they favourable?'

'He showed promise of being a worthy opponent for a few days, at least. He prepared himself quite thoroughly, I believe.'

'There was no arrangement between you and Darrell, or between the trainers, as to how the race should be conducted?'

Chadwick inhaled loudly and ominously. He did not like the implication in the question.

'Sergeant, I have no need of prior arrangements with pedestrians who challenge me. I am a serious athlete. However, I believe that my man Harvey mentioned an approach being made by Darrell's trainer early on Tuesday morning. You will have to ask Harvey about that.'

'Thank you, I shall.'

'Is that all then? I *am* at present trying to engage in a race, you know.'

'Two other questions, sir. Do you by any chance take any form of stimulant to aid your performance?'

'If you are asking whether I am in the practice of swallowing strychnine, the answer is no. The only chemical that you will find in that cupboard – and you may look if you wish – is a Seidlitz powder, which I imagine even you may find a necessary aperient on occasions. What is your other question?'

'A personal one, sir. It's important I know the answer, though. If you win this race you take the prize of five hundred pounds. But as a man of fortune you'll have staked some money on the result, I expect. How much will you collect on Saturday, sir?'

Chadwick was on the point of refusing to answer, but Cribb's final sentence, with its dismissal of the threat from O'Flaherty was a disarming touch.

'I don't see how it affects your investigation. However, the answer is eleven thousand pounds.'

*

The method. It was useless trying to prevent the next murder without isolating a probable method. Poisoning and gassing had been used; they could not be discounted, but it was likelier that the murderer would vary his style again. A stabbing? Unlikely: that was too crude and too immediate for this stamp of killer. His was the insidious approach. His crimes were open to interpretation as suicides, or accidents. He was no sledgehammer maniac, as O'Flaherty pictured him.

Mostyn-Smith had spent the morning devising, and dismissing, theories. They had so preoccupied him that he walked for six minutes longer than his schedule allowed, time that he could ill-afford. He had decided, in his thoughtful circumambulations, to sacrifice a portion of his next rest-period and examine O'Flaherty's new hut. There, surely, was where the murderer would bait his trap. The Irishman had not left the track for lunch before one o'clock on any of the previous days, so it should be possible to make a careful inspection without being disturbed.

He permitted himself twenty minutes in his own hut, resting his legs and eating fruit and honey. This was not a rest-period when he planned to sleep.

By now he had decided that the method would have to be some form of poisoning, after all. Strychnine, of course, was unlikely, but there were so many alternative methods. It was essential to get into O'Flaherty's hut and examine everything that was consumable. His training in medicine had taught him that most known poisons were detectable, by smell or because they were not completely soluble. Any food or drink that appeared at all doubtful he would destroy. The Irishman might not thank him for doing it, but his conscience would at least be clear.

It was time. He wrapped the apple-peelings and core in paper that he kept for the purpose, straightened the bedding and left the hut. Then he dropped the refuse into a bin outside, noting that it had not been emptied for twenty-four hours. He walked to the back of the huts, towards the ablutions area, taking care that anyone watching would not guess at his intentions. When he was quite sure everything was quiet he moved round O'Flaherty's hut towards the front. At the corner of the building he stopped short. The door was opening from the inside. And O'Flaherty was still on the track.

Mostyn-Smith backed out of sight. Furtively, the trespasser quit the hut, and moved away at speed towards the arena. There was no mistaking who it was.

Constable Thackeray found Cribb in the police office.

'Mind if I sit down, Sarge? I've been on my feet since six.'

'Good man,' said Cribb from a well-cushioned swivel-chair.

Thackeray decided not to press the matter of his fatigue. He had been tramping the London streets because the fog outside had slowed everything, trams, buses and cabs, to less than walking pace. Cribb would not be unsympathetic, but the temptation to make some comparison with the tramp going on inside the Hall would be irresistible. So Thackeray suffered his aching feet without any more comment.

'You've got the search organized for the chemist?' Cribb inquired.

172

'The order's been passed round, Sarge. The operation should be fully under way by now. The fog won't help us, though. It's a job getting any sort of message through in this.'

'Quite so. How d'you get on at Highbury?'

'Now that's really going to interest you,' said Thackeray confidently. 'They was nice people. Honest folk, I'd judge, but they'd cover up for Mrs D. if they thought she was in trouble.'

'You didn't give 'em that impression, I hope.'

'I did not.' Thackeray was slightly affronted. 'I established that she was with them yesterday afternoon, and then I inquired when they had seen her previous to that. They was both quite firm about it – man and wife, middle-aged couple. They hadn't seen Cora since the week before, on Thursday. It's a weekly arrangement.'

'Is it, by Jove? Nice work! You asked about Monday evening?'

'Yes. They was at the Lyceum, watching Irving in some play about Venice.'

'She lied then. Why should she have done that? Wonder where she really got to that evening.'

14

'**D**ay and a half to go. Better spend lunch-time on the case.'

Cribb's announcement at first depressed Thackeray, who did not usually fast on Fridays, or any other day. But he brightened when the proposal became clearer. They were to discuss their findings over battered fish in the Hall restaurant.

It was nearly two o'clock, so they had the room almost to themselves.

'Trouble with this lot,' said Cribb, 'is the lies.' His usual staccato utterances were separated by periods of chewing. 'Too many folk with things to hide.'

'Mrs Darrell, you mean, Sarge?'

'Her, yes. And Monk, when he was alive.' He scooped more cod into his mouth. 'Chadwick, too. Makes out he's confident. Poor bastard's terrified of losing to a scrubber.'

Thackeray took up the theme.

'Come to that, Herriott's not all lavender. He grew a trifle warm when it looked like we'd have to call off the race, didn't he?'

174

'Hm. There's Jacobson as well. Halfway up Carey Street if my bookie friend's right.' Cribb put down his fork. 'Point is, Thackeray, can you call any of these a motive for two murders? You don't think so? I don't. We're looking for something else. Maybe someone else.'

'Possibly one of the runners, Sarge. That doctor bloke could get his hands on strychnine without being asked any questions.'

Cribb was dubious.

'What does he gain from killing off Darrell and Monk? Stands no chance of winning.'

'Ah,' said Thackeray, brandishing a knife authoritatively, 'but who *does* now? O'Flaherty could very well beat Chadwick tomorrow. He's been gaining for days. One thing I've noticed is that nobody takes more interest in that Irishman than the little doctor.'

'So Mostyn-Smith takes a cut from Paddy's winnings? It's plausible, Thackeray, it's plausible. Far as I can discover, it was Mostyn-Smith that got the tetanus scare started.'

The constable nodded sagely. The more they considered it, the better his theory seemed.

'Two things don't fit,' said Cribb. 'If the Doc killed Monk why crack him on the head? Too crude for a medical man. And if it was O'Flaherty that clonked him, why report the gas escape?'

'That's the cunning of the Irish, Sarge.'

Cribb shook his head.

'Not for my money. Nothing deep about our Dublin friend. No, Thackeray. Time we finished with theories. Let's stick to facts.'

The constable returned to his meal. If Cribb wanted to work with facts that was his business. But Thackeray was privately convinced that the same facts would lead them to his own two suspects.

'Take Darrell's murder first,' Cribb went on. 'We agree someone fixed the bracer after Monk brought it here. Must have got into the tent. Right. Tent's in full view of everybody. Couldn't be more central. So what time's the best?'

'When there's no crowd, Sarge.'

'Correct. Now, right from the start the Press are about. Crowd begins arriving at first light. Eyes on the tents all the time, you see. People come and go, too, looking in the tent. Herriott and the Press. Cora Darrell and Monk. When's our poisoner going to get in there?'

Thackeray saw the point.

'He must have waited till near midnight, when the crowd had left, but while Darrell was still on the track. The light would be poorer then, too.'

'Fine. All he has to look out for is Monk. Now suppose Monk goes off for a drink. He liked his liquor. Our poisoner gets into the tent with time to do what he wants. Poor perishers on the track wouldn't notice much. He can slip in when Darrell's round the other side of the track.'

'That lets out Mrs Darrell, don't it?'

'Not really,' said Cribb. 'But if she puts in the crystals it's done in the afternoon. Monk has to be an accomplice. Motive's there, of course. Kill the old man and make off with your lover.'

'I'd have gone for that until Monk was killed,' reflected

Thackeray. 'But that changed everything. She wouldn't want to fix Monk.'

'Except when she knew they'd both swing for it,' said Cribb caustically. 'I wouldn't count her out yet.' He pushed away the now-empty plate. 'Now let's talk about Monk's murder. When was he bashed, d'you think?'

'Wednesday night—' Thackeray's eyes widened in realization. 'About midnight, Sarge. The same blinking time!'

Cribb received this observation with a patient nod.

'May be significant. May not. Now what I need to know— What's that?'

Shouts were coming from the main Hall, shouts that were loud to penetrate to where they were. And these were not jeers or roars of encouragement. There were voices raised in alarm, and screams.

'Someone's in trouble!' Cribb jerked to attention, and the chair behind him overturned with the vigour of his movement. He stood listening.

A voice in the Hall clearly called, 'Get a doctor!'

The sergeant moved at an astonishing rate. He had cursed himself the day before for being out of the Hall when Monk was murdered. If another crime had been committed ... He ran from the restaurant, and the door swung into Thackeray as he lumbered after.

The Hall was not very full, but it rang with shouts – of concern, anger, panic. The uproar was directed at a small group on the opposite side of the track. Dodging between passing competitors, Cribb sprinted across the centre, and forced his way through the close-packed officials.

Mostyn-Smith was kneeling by the jack-knifed body

of O'Flaherty, who lay groaning in obvious distress. Timekeepers, reporters and others leaned over them, demanding information, urging advice. Cribb acted decisively.

'Police!' he shouted in a voice that silenced even the Press. 'Doctor, can this man be moved?'

Mostyn-Smith spoke without looking up.

'He is trying to speak. I cannot help him unless I can hear what he says. Will you all kindly go away?'

The request was futile, and Cribb realized it. Already the babel around O'Flaherty had restarted. The sergeant touched the arms of two burly officials.

'Help us get him to that tent.'

He yanked Mostyn-Smith to his feet and to one side as though he were a straying child. Then he stooped to O'Flaherty and with the help of Thackeray and the others lifted him to the tent that Darrell had used when he was alive. When the still-groaning Irishman was deposited on the mattress inside, Cribb waved out the others and instructed Thackeray to stand guard.

'You can let the Doc in. No one else.'

Mostyn-Smith was admitted. His face was eloquent of affronted dignity, but his generous shorts over legs like lamp-standards rather undermined the effect. He ignored Cribb, and went to the patient. O'Flaherty was speaking:

'Couldn't go on. My feet . . . burning. Can't understand it. Never had trouble like this.'

Mostyn-Smith unlaced the boots, pulled off the socks and examined the runner's feet. They were red and

178

swollen, but so were his own, as anyone's would be after five days of walking.

'Do you have any additional pains? Are your muscles at all troublesome?'

'Not really. I'm stiff, but I expect to be. It's the bloody feet. God in Heaven, what's happening to them?'

Cribb was examining one of the discarded boots, feeling inside it.

'Got another pair of boots, have you?'

'Yes,' answered O'Flaherty.

'And socks?'

'I think so.'

'Good. I'm no doctor but I'll give you my advice. Soak your feet in salt water. Get on those other socks and boots, and double back to the track. You're losing all the ground you gained.'

'I must protest!' Mostyn-Smith rounded on Cribb. 'You have no authority whatsoever to override me in this way. I am a qualified practitioner and I intend to examine this man with the professional expertise—'

'Please yourself,' snapped Cribb. 'I'll save you both a bit of time if you take my advice. Look at this.' He upended the boot that he was holding. A spray of sand-like grains flowed from it into his cupped right hand.

'There's your irritant. You've been nobbled, my friend. Some party slipped this inside your boots.'

O'Flaherty sat up, suddenly rallied.

'Let me see.'

Cribb tipped some of the substance into the Irishman's palm. He examined it, turning it over with his finger-tips.

179

'By Jesus! I know what this is!' blurted O'Flaherty, suddenly on his feet.

'Sit down, man!' ordered Cribb, pushing him in the chest, so that he sank back on to the bed. 'You'll still have some embedded in your soles.'

'Crushed walnut shells!' exclaimed the disgusted pedestrian. 'The oldest bloody trick going, and I fell for it. Who would have done this?'

'Anyone who didn't want you to win,' Cribb answered drily.

Mostyn-Smith was suddenly too interested to continue his display of pique.

'May I see this? You say that it is manufactured by crushing walnut shells?'

As Mostyn-Smith peered at the tiny fragments which had been handed over, O'Flaherty jerked at Thackeray's sleeve.

'Do me a favour, bobby. Ask one of those reporters to bring me a bucket of water. I've got to get back.' Cribb nodded his approval of this arrangement.

'If the doctor doesn't mind?'

'No, no,' concurred Mostyn-Smith. 'Please carry on. This abrasive is unquestionably responsible for your collapse, O'Flaherty.'

The Irishman treated the diagnosis with contempt. He was preoccupied in extracting minute chips of shell from his inflamed soles. But at Cribb's voice he looked up.

'When did you put these boots on?'

'One o'clock. I had a bite, and changed my footgear. I keep a spare pair, you see.'

'You don't share a hut now, do you?'

'No. I've one to myself.'

'Anyone else been in there?'

'If I found anyone there, I'd—' His eyes lighted on Mostyn-Smith. 'You were there! You came into my hut, waking me up this morning. This is the bloody man, Sergeant! Take him away and lock him up! Saints in Heaven, I've been sleeping with a murderer!'

'One moment,' began Mostyn-Smith. 'I can assure—'

'Take a look at that portmanteau in his hut!' O'Flaherty continued. 'It's stuffed full of bottles and boxes. Strychnine you're looking for? It's there, I'll stake my soul on it! Take him away, Sergeant. No man's safe while he's at liberty.'

Thackeray's eyes were gaping at this tirade. If the Irishman's accusations were true, then his own suspicions about Mostyn-Smith were justified. But his theory had not included an attempt to cripple O'Flaherty.

Cribb addressed Mostyn-Smith.

'Is this right? Did you go to this man's hut this morning?'

Mostyn-Smith's indignation was such that he found difficulty in expressing himself.

'I did – that is to say – Sergeant – you cannot believe—'

'What did you want with Mr O'Flaherty, sir?'

He took a deep breath, visibly taking control of his emotions. 'I felt that it was my duty to warn him of possible dangers. He is not a percipient individual, Sergeant—'

'You—' O'Flaherty made a grab for Mostyn-Smith which Cribb sharply repulsed with a downward thrust of his arm.

181

'Keep out of this!'

Distraction was provided at that moment. Thackeray took in the bucket of water from outside. It was placed in front of O'Flaherty and he sulkily planted a foot inside it, and began massaging the toes under the water.

Mostyn-Smith resumed his explanation.

'I felt obliged to warn him of the dangers to which he was exposed, as the only possible rival to Captain Chadwick. I reasoned that whoever had killed poor Darrell would not balk at murdering anyone else who threatened to overtake the Captain. I therefore approached this – man to acquaint him with my fears. I roused him before four o'clock and we conversed about the matter.'

Cribb turned to O'Flaherty.

'Is this true?'

O'Flaherty nodded morosely. Cribb turned back to Mostyn-Smith.

'You didn't touch the boots?'

'I do not even remember seeing them.'

'And you didn't go into the hut again, after Mr O'Flaherty had left for the track?'

There was the slightest hesitation before he answered firmly, 'I did not.'

Cribb did not let it pass.

'You planned to go there?'

'Yes – to check that nobody had tampered with his food and drink, but I changed my mind.'

'Why was that?'

Another pause.

'It might have seemed like trespassing.'

Cribb turned to another point.

'This portmanteau—'

'I thought you would want to know about that. I freely admit that it contains a number of bottles, phials and boxes of pills. These are my personal needs, Sergeant. You may certainly have them analyzed if you wish, but I must warn you that if you choose to take them away from me at this stage I shall require substantial compensation.'

Cribb was puzzled.

'I don't follow you.'

The little man took on a superior air.

'That is understandable, Sergeant. My appearance in this endurance contest has been much commented on in the popular journals. People are curious to know why an educated person should engage in a pedestrian contest against the dubious fraternity who make a living out of such affairs. I make no claims to athletic prowess. Before last August I had not walked more than five miles at one stretch in my life. You see, Sergeant, I am interested in physiological research. You might say that my participation is in the nature of an experiment.'

'What are you proving?' asked Cribb sceptically.

'Ah! That is the explanation of my portmanteau. Inside it are more than fifty healthful foods and drinks of my own concoction. They, with an occasional fruit, are all that I consume on my journey. They banish the effect of fatigue entirely, by nourishing the system, recharging the natural—'

'And you plan to sell them under an advertisement of yourself in running-costume,' Cribb broke in, cutting

183

short the explanation. 'Neat idea, if you do any good in the race.'

'I shall, if I am permitted to continue,' said Mostyn-Smith.

'And you shall!' announced Cribb, to O'Flaherty's undisguised fury. 'I'll take a look at these bottles, if you don't object, but we'll leave them in your hut. A piece of advice, though. Say nothing about the walnut shells. Keep away from this man, and if you have any suspicions tell 'em to us.'

'I shall indeed,' Mostyn-Smith readily pledged. He delved into his shorts and from somewhere produced a gold watch. 'I have lost some twenty-five minutes. May I now return to the track?'

Cribb gave his assent, and the doctor-detective pocketed the watch and scuttled like the March Hare through the flap that Thackeray held open.

'That's a murderer!' O'Flaherty blurted out. 'He tried to poison me—'

'You didn't say that,' snapped Cribb. 'Did he give you any food or drink?'

'Well, no.'

'Did he warn you of possible danger?'

'Yes, but—'

'Hold your tongue, then!' snapped Cribb. 'You'll need all the strength you've got left to catch Chadwick. Thackeray, fetch his spare boots and socks. They're lying somewhere in the hut, are they? We'll check them before he puts 'em on. And for God's sake, O'Flaherty, take care what you eat and drink.'

184

As Thackeray left there was a general move from the bystanders to gain admittance. Cribb stood squarely at the entrance and addressed them.

'If you'll be silent, gentlemen? Thank you. Mr O'Flaherty will shortly return to the track. He stopped because his feet were inflamed. They've now been soaked and he's in better shape. In justice, gentlemen, let him get back to the track as soon as possible. He hasn't the time to answer questions.'

The bubble had been pricked. In disappointment, the reporters began to disperse. Several hopefully questioned Cribb on the murder, but he declined to comment. Inside the tent O'Flaherty hastily prepared to set off again after Chadwick. Thackeray soon returned with the boots and socks and without more words being spoken the Stag put them on and quit the tent.

'Probably scotched any chance he had,' commented Cribb, as they watched him set off again. 'Walnut shells! We've picked up a wrinkle or two these last few days.'

'He'll never catch Chadwick now,' agreed Thackeray. 'Been going like a three year old this last hour. They might as well hand him the prize tonight, and then everyone could get home for a decent sleep.'

'Leaving us without our killer,' Cribb added sardonically.

'Do you reckon the walnut-shell merchant is the same one?' asked Thackeray.

'Could be. It lets out Cora Darrell if that's the case. She's not been in here since the night Monk was killed. May be a false trail, though. Mustn't lose sight of the real matter – the killings.'

185

'Don't you think it's worth finding out who nobbled O'Flaherty, Sarge?'

Cribb breathed out noisily in some impatience.

'I thought I'd made it clear. We're on the look-out for a killer. Not a bloody fixer of races. If it turns out to be the same party, that's fine. But I'm not cutting into a murder inquiry to chase a nut-cracking oddboy. Understand?'

Thackeray understood. None the less he was personally convinced that there was a better chance of clearing up the main case if they could solve this lesser mystery. Sergeant Cribb was well known for the number of successful inquiries he had conducted, yet there *had* been occasion when he had acted precipitately. But for these blemishes on an impressive record he might have risen higher by now ... Mindful of his own rank, Thackeray kept his thoughts to himself.

The detectives walked back towards the track in silence. Thackeray had needled Cribb. He knew that nothing he said would help matters until the mood passed. Cribb, in turn, was laconic; not because he was studying Thackeray. He was mentally re-examining each suspect, searching for the motive he felt certain was waiting to be detected.

The silence was disturbed by a third person. As they waited indecisively at the track edge, watching O'Flaherty's new display of energy, Mostyn-Smith reappeared a little breathlessly at their side.

'You will forgive me, gentlemen? There is something else that I should tell you. I hesitated about mentioning the matter when our Irish friend was present, because I seriously feared that he might be incited to violence.'

He peered about him, ensuring that he could not be overheard. As they were inside the ropes at the end of the track farthest from the timekeepers there was no fear of eavesdroppers.

'I believe that I know who tampered with O'Flaherty's boots,' he muttered confidentially. 'At about midday – or twenty-seven minutes past to be specific – I approached his hut with a view to checking that his food and drink had not been poisoned. I had deduced that the murderer would attack O'Flaherty next, you understand, and it seemed to be obvious that he would employ some form of poisoning again. I approached the hut from the rear, and as I turned from the side of the building I saw someone come out of the hut, and move quickly away to the track.'

'You recognized him?'

'Most certainly. It was that trainer-fellow who works for Captain Chadwick.'

'Harvey?'

'That's correct. He is plainly the perpetrator of these crimes.'

15

The Press accounts of the race had followed a well-established pattern. For the first day or two it was described as the 'Islington Mix'; by the third day, 'Herriott's Wobble'; and at the end of the week the 'Cruelty Show at the Agricultural Hall'. As the eventual result became more certain, reports dwelt instead on the state of the blistered survivors. And the more harrowing the details, the larger the attendance. Londoners by the thousand flocked to Islington through fog and sodden streets as Romans once converged on the Colosseum.

In fact, the scenes on this Friday evening were less distressing than they had been on the previous Monday, before an altogether smaller audience. Those remaining on the track were mostly experienced pedestrians, the 'distance brigade', veterans of many campaigns. But in the race's early stages there were novices to this type of race. Their greenness had been painfully evident after only a few hours. The one notable 'tenderfoot' to keep going was Billy Reid. By now he was half a day's walking down on the leaders, but his spirit was indomitable.

'A bloody sight pluckier than most lads,' was Chalk's comment, as he and Williams watched Billy hobbling back to the track from the tents. 'When I'm done with this caper, and sets up as trainer, that's the mettle of lad I want. 'E's the wrong shape for a stayer, of course. You can't carry too much top 'amper for very long. But blimey, 'e's no namby-pamby.'

'That's true,' agreed the Half-breed. 'See some of them characters weeping buckets after only ten hours? Don't matter 'ow pretty a man's shape is. You can't do nothing with a party that pipes 'is eye.'

'Beats me 'ow 'e does it, with that brother of 'is badgering 'im all bloody day. 'E give 'im an 'ot bath this morning to liven 'im up. Fairly made the boy sing out, that did. If any bloody trainer tried that with me I'd land one on 'im, I tell you.'

'Never agreed with bathin' meself,' Williams confided. 'Softens the soles of your feet, that does.'

The main interest on the track that evening was provided by Chadwick and O'Flaherty, who moved at a positive trot, the Irishman within a yard of the Captain. But the pace was being set, surprisingly, by Mostyn-Smith, determined to win back his lost time. This trio remained locked for lap upon lap, and the crowd urged them noisily to go faster, desperately hoping that one of the two leaders, both heavily backed, would crack. For the rest of the field it was a challenge to keep upright, mobile and awake. None had the strength or inclination to 'mix'.

'Nippy on his feet for a nark,' Williams remarked, indicating Mostyn-Smith. "E'll bloody lick us on this showing. What's 'e going full bat for? Still another ruddy day to go.'

''E's no nark,' Chalk corrected him contemptuously. 'Bloody crank. That's what 'e is.'

'I seen 'im talking with the Law,' maintained Williams. 'That's no ped. I never saw 'im on a track before in my life.'

'You ask Feargus about 'im, mate. 'E reckons Double-barrel fixed Charlie Darrell and Sam Monk, and 'ad a go at 'im.'

'Feargus!' Williams spat generously over his shoulder, not bothering to see who was following. 'Squint-eyed bloody Irishman! Thinks anyone that comes near 'im's after 'is blood.'

'Come off it. O'Flaherty's pretty near 'im right now. 'E don't mind using 'im as pacemaker.'

'Don't you believe it,' said Williams. 'Only one reason why Feargus keeps close behind Double-barrel. Makes sure that way 'e won't get stabbed in the back!' They trudged on, amused, but a shade embittered by their colleague's single-minded efforts. Earlier they had enjoyed delaying Chadwick so that O'Flaherty could gain ground. Now that the Irishman aspired to honours they felt resentful without admitting it to each other.

There were hoots of delighted derision from the stands as a portly figure in an overcoat joined the leading trio. It was Thackeray, as unmistakable a member of the Force as one of Punch's plain-clothes constables. He had been instructed to talk with Chadwick, and since Chadwick had no intention of leaving the track, Thackeray had to conduct another interview in motion, only in less discreet circumstances than his last one. He could scarcely make himself audible above the whistles and mock applause as he lengthened his stride to keep pace with the leaders. A well-aimed apple dislodged his bowler and he snatched vainly in the air for it as it fell to the track. He decided to keep going without it.

'Mr – Captain Chadwick, sir.'

Chadwick inclined his head towards him, but said nothing.

'I'm Constable Thackeray, sir, of the detective police.'

There was no comment, so he went on, between gasps for breath.

'I think – you may be able – to assist us, sir.'

Chadwick did not look as though he intended to.

'Your trainer—'

'I do not employ a trainer,' Chadwick observed icily. 'I presume that you mean my assistant.'

'Mr Harvey, sir.'

'Yes.'

'We can't find him – sir. The Sergeant – wants to question him.'

'Isn't he in my tent?'

'No, sir.'

'Then I cannot help you. I have no idea where he can be. I am not a detective.'

Thackeray drew up, and the crowd feigned a unified howl of disappointment. He ignored them, and walked back to retrieve his hat before it was trampled upon.

Sergeant Cribb had denied himself a second look at Thackeray in action. Time was desperately short, so he had sought out Sol Herriott while Thackeray performed for the crowd. The promoter was in his office with Jacobson, checking the previous day's takings.

'You don't mind, sir?' Cribb asked Jacobson. 'A few discreet inquiries, you understand.' He was already on his way out, characteristically withdrawing at the first opportunity. He nodded at Cribb, and left.

'Doing well, sir?' Cribb asked.

Herriott replaced the coin-bags in the safe, turned his ample frame and faced the sergeant. On the wall behind him were oleographs of Smithfield prize fatstock.

'Yes, all things considered,' he cautiously replied.

'Good crowd in there tonight. Best yet.'

'So I believe.'

'Funny really, you know. Got a killer loose in there somewhere but it don't keep the crowd away.'

'Evidently not,' said Herriott. 'Do you smoke?'

Cribb did not, except as a tactical gesture.

'Thanks. I wanted to get my mind clear about last Monday,' he said. 'Thought if I came to see you I'd get a good account of what people were doing the evening before Darrell was killed.'

'I'll try to help.'

'Fine. Chadwick first. I suppose he was on the track all the time.'

'Oh yes,' Herriott remembered. 'And he was running, to everyone's surprise. He has always walked every yard of the way before.'

'He kept going till one o'clock?'

'Yes. I'm sure of that. Darrell went to his tent at the same time.'

'Good. Now Harvey, the trainer. What was he doing?'

'Ah. He would have been attending Chadwick. He doesn't often leave his side. He's probably under orders to be constantly in attendance. A soldier has to take his orders seriously.'

'He wasn't in the tent, then?'

'I don't think so. He followed the race closely from the trackside.'

Cribb tapped his cigar on the silver ash-tray on Herriott's desk.

'Now what about Mr Jacobson, sir? Where was he?'

Herriott reflected. His waistcoat front started quivering over his belly at some amusing recollection.

'Poor old Walter! Yes, he was here, Sergeant.'

'What's amusing you?'

'Well, I dined out earlier in the evening, and left Jacobson in charge. He's not exactly a man who welcomes responsibility, you know. Before I left I jokingly told him what to do if a fire started. Damned if we didn't get one in the kitchen! Small affair, but it ruined his evening – and his suit, I may say.'

'What time was this?'

'Ten o'clock, approximately.'

'And you returned . . . ?'

'A few minutes after midnight.'

'Where did you have your dinner, sir? Pardon the question. I must know everyone's whereabouts.'

'At my club – the London Sporting.'

'And you dined alone?'

'Yes.'

193

Cribb turned to another matter.

'I'd like to ask you about the way this race was first arranged, sir.'

'Certainly,' beamed Herriott. 'What do you want to know?'

'Well, sir.' Cribb drew deeply on the cigar, and extinguished it with great thoroughness before going on. 'What interests me is that you are not known as a promoter of foot-races. You're more of a turf man, I believe.'

'That's so.'

'It must have meant quite a gamble, organizing this affair.'

'In a way, yes,' Herriott agreed. 'But I'm a gambling man, too, you know. And, of course, this isn't the first six-day race. It has been done very successfully before.'

'What puzzles me, Mr Herriott, is why you employed a man like Jacobson as your manager. I hear that he knows no more about pedestrianism than you do. Why didn't you take on a man who knows the game?'

'Aren't you impressed with my manager?' Herriott asked, with a smile. 'Now, Sergeant, you mustn't take my earlier remarks about him too seriously. Walter's a competent fellow. Just a little reserved.'

'You've employed him before, have you?'

'Oh yes, in a similar capacity, a long while back. But really, you know, the job's a sinecure. I do most of the managing myself, as you may have observed.'

'Why take on Jacobson at all, then?'

Herriott shrugged.

'I need to get away occasionally, Sergeant, and there

194

must be somebody in attendance throughout. It's the kind of post that one gives to an old friend.'

'—who's fallen on hard times?'

'Did I imply that?' asked Herriott. 'Well, one likes to offer help where one can.'

'You know Mr Jacobson is in debt, then?'

Herriott sighed.

'I had a shrewd suspicion that he was in financial trouble. I didn't inquire about it. One doesn't, unless the information is volunteered.'

'Quite so.'

'I ought to say,' Herriott added, 'that both Jacobson and I made a close study of six-day events before we embarked on this enterprise. And I think you'll agree that the race has been a success, a well-matched affair, in spite of Darrell's unfortunate death.'

'How did you persuade Captain Chadwick to enter?' Cribb asked, ignoring the last remark. 'He's not one of the Hackney Wick fraternity.'

'Ah!' Herriott was smiling proudly. 'Privileged information, Sergeant. A friend of mine happened to know that he wanted to test himself over six days but couldn't face the prospect of mingling with a batch of peds. The separate tracks were my inspiration.'

'You didn't know him before this, then?'

'No, Sergeant. Fellow's not really my type.'

'Mine neither. As a matter of interest, sir, d'you know anything about this man, Harvey?'

'Harvey? Oh, the trainer! He was his batman, wasn't he? No, I know very little of him. He seems very capable.'

'Yes.' Cribb smiled at an undisclosed thought. 'Well, sir. Thank you for your time. You've been helpful.'

'I like to be, if I can,' Herriott gushed.

'The race finishes at ten-thirty Saturday night, I believe.'

'That's so.'

'You'll make some kind of presentation to the winners?'

Herriott leaned back and tapped the safe.

'I've over a thousand pounds in here, Sergeant, and a magnificent belt. Oh yes, I'll have a presentation ceremony on Saturday night – if the winner can walk up for his prize, of course!' He was convulsed with laughter at the prospect of a champion too exhausted to cover another step. 'I hope you'll be there to see it, Sergeant.'

'Looks as though I shall, sir,' Cribb confirmed, without much enthusiasm.

Thackeray was waiting in some perturbation for Cribb to leave Herriott's office.

'I've looked everywhere I know, Sarge. Harvey just ain't to be found.'

'You've asked Chadwick?'

'He don't seem interested.'

'Don't suppose he will be before one o'clock. Harvey should be here by then. Strict on their duties, these military men. Now how about the strychnine hunt? Any reports come in?'

If they had, Thackeray had been too preoccupied to collect them from the police office. The two detectives walked in that direction, past the arena, which had filled almost to capacity. Mostyn-Smith, rather redder in the face now, was still a yard in front of Chadwick, with

O'Flaherty almost at his side. The strain was telling on all three. They clung to the pace more in desperation than determination. Whoever succumbed now would be mentally accepting defeat.

The constable on duty had a sheaf of papers ready for Cribb. He thumped them through rapidly, rejecting many, and then examined the rest more carefully.

'No help here,' he finally told Thackeray. 'We'll get some more in tomorrow. I'm not too confident though. Seems another dead end.'

'Should we see Mrs Darrell again, and face her with the false statement about where she was last Monday evening?'

'Not much point. I don't think she'll tell us much that we don't know. Now what's this? Ah!'

He picked up a report that he had at first rejected.

'Our chemist, Sarge?'

'No. The report on Monk's note. I wanted the hand-writing analyzed, compared with his signature in the poison-book.'

'What's their view, then?' asked Thackeray.

'As I thought, unfortunately. Monk definitely wrote the letter. No shadow of doubt.'

Thackeray was mystified.

'I don't follow, Sarge. That was a suicide note – *must* have been cooked up by the killer.'

Cribb shook his head. His constable had disappointed him again.

'Not so, not so! Got a note of the wording of that note, have you?'

Thackeray embarrassedly delved for his notebook. He

197

read out Monk's message. '"This is to show how sorry I am. I did not mean him to die. Samuel Monk." – Was he forced to write it, do you think, Sarge?'

'Not very likely. Poor fellow was too drunk to write anything, by Jacobson's account. No. What we've got to work out is *when* he wrote it, Thackeray. That's the key.'

Thackeray remained bewildered.

'It don't make any sort of sense, to me, Sarge. If Monk didn't kill Darrell – and we know that he couldn't have – why should he take the blame on himself? He was so sure of himself that night when we saw him in the tent. He *knew* his bracer had been mixed right.'

'Of course he did!' said Cribb. 'So he couldn't have taken the blame. You're right. But give a thought to the timing, man. There was a time when Monk would have had a guilty conscience.'

'I still don't—'

'Before he knew it was strychnine that killed Darrell! What did they think it was at first?'

'Tetanus, Sarge.'

'Right. And how do you contract tetanus?'

'Through getting something into a wound – like the cow dung this place stinks of.'

'Exactly. Well, there's the point. Darrell ran barefoot on blistered feet that Monday night, and Monk didn't stop him. Wouldn't he feel responsible and write a note like this?'

'You mean he planned to kill himself then, Sarge?'

'I didn't say that. But that's when he wrote it.'

'Who to?'

'Ain't that obvious?'

Thackeray was not sure that it was, but prudently nodded agreement.

Harvey re-entered the Hall carrying a paper parcel soon after eleven that evening. He was instantly recognized by the constable on duty at the Islington Green gate and hustled to the police office where Cribb and Thackeray were waiting.

'Thought you'd walked out on us, Mr Harvey,' Cribb began. 'Couldn't find you anywhere. Not like you to leave Captain Chadwick to his own devices.'

'I had good reason,' answered Harvey.

'No doubt of that, no doubt at all. You know why we want to talk with you?'

'I'm not sure.'

'I'll not wrap it in fancy words then. You were seen leaving O'Flaherty's hut this morning. Later on he pulled out of the race with sore feet. Crushed nutshells. Do you admit putting them in his boots?' Harvey was admirably calm.

'I did it, yes.'

'Why then?'

'Ain't you worked that out, Sergeant? I'm on Captain Chadwick's side, in case you don't remember.'

'Don't you play smart with me,' warned Cribb. 'You might be in a lot of trouble.'

'What's the charge, then?' asked Harvey confidently. 'Trespassing – or assault?'

'Could be a double charge of murder,' Cribb answered, and Harvey's manner changed at once.

'You think that I – because I got at O'Flaherty's boots – oh no, Sergeant! That ain't true!'

'You've got a clearer motive for killing Darrell than anyone in this Hall,' said Cribb. 'Your actions confirm you'll take big chances to see Chadwick win. You care nothing for O'Flaherty. You'd cripple him for Chadwick's sake. Why shouldn't you have poisoned Darrell? Could have slipped in more strychnine than you meant, of course. Murder is deliberate, with malice afore-thought. Might make it manslaughter on the first charge. If you'll cough the full story—'

'Look, I'm no murderer!' protested Harvey. 'I know nothing about Darrell's death, or Monk's. I've admitted fixing the Irishman's boots, but that don't make me a killer.'

Cribb pressed his advantage.

'You'd better talk pretty quick, then, Mr Harvey. I want to know all about you and your gaffer, and I want to know your movements last Monday night. You'd better remember it right too. I've been given several accounts of that night, and I know what happened most of the time.'

Harvey collected his thoughts. Last Monday seemed an age ago. Thackeray took out his notebook.

'Far as I can recall,' Harvey began, 'I was by the track all evening, following the race. The Captain was behaving strange-like – he was running, you see. He has always walked his races, even when the articles allow mixing. But he fell badly behind Darrell that first day. Even some of the slow mob were ahead of him and by two in the afternoon he'd taken to running. Now I knew this running would give him no end of trouble—'

'Why didn't you stop it, then?'

'Stop it? I can't stop the Captain. He don't take orders from me, or anyone, come to that. No, I just had to be around in case he went down with cramp. There was some bad collapses that first day. Once a man's gone down it's a sure bet that others will follow.'

'So you waited for the collapse.'

'Well, I kept near, in case. As it happened, he suffered a bit, but he didn't go down. And he won back a lot of the ground. Darrell was in some kind of trouble with his feet, and that gave a fillip to the Captain. He kept going until Darrell came off at one, and then we both went into the tent.'

'What sort of mental state was he in?'

'Mental?'

'His state of mind, man. Was he happy?'

'Oh no. Far from it. He was suffering. Very sore, he was, and right low in spirits. Not like the Captain at all. He's always enjoyed his walking, you know. But this time he was talking of giving up. After one day!'

'Did he eat anything?' asked Cribb.

Harvey tried to remember.

'I don't think so. He took his usual glass of claret, though, and then I left him.'

'Where did you go?'

'To the restaurant. I needed a drink, and there's benches in there where a man can stretch out for a couple of hours.'

'And that's what you did?'

'Well,' answered Harvey. 'I didn't get the drink. They'd

201

had some kind of trouble in the kitchen – a fire, I think – and nobody was around to serve. So I found myself a corner and kipped for a bit. I finally got some coffee about three-thirty. Oh yes, and Monk came in.'

'Monk? You're sure of the time?'

'Yes, about three-thirty. He sat with me. He must have just come in from outside because he was darned cold. Funny thing, he wanted to fix something up with me. He thought the pace was too warm. If I would hold the Captain back he'd tell Darrell to take things easy. I wouldn't have it though. I can't give orders to the Captain like some of them trainers do with their guv'nors. So it was no deal. And blow me, when they got back on track bloody Darrell set off like a hare before hounds.'

'Full of strychnine,' commented Cribb. 'Did Monk say anything else?'

'No. That was the lot,' answered Harvey.

'Right. Tell us about the Captain now. How long have you been with him?'

'Must be ten years, at least. I served in India with him, you know. He wasn't walking professional then, of course. Only started that when we got back home, about five years back. Then it was strictly private matches, on the road. Pretty soon he was taking on the best of England and showing them clean heels. He wanted to meet Darrell, of course, and that's how he came to enlist in this tail-chasing squad. Darrell wouldn't face him on the open road. Said he was prepared to take him on at Islington though. Then it was up to Herriott to arrange the twin tracks. My guv'nor wouldn't risk his feet among that

202

hobnailed mob – not until he was forced to join 'em, of course. He had no choice after Darrell was out.'

'So I heard. But he'll net a tidy sum in bets for his troubles.'

'I wouldn't know about that. He puts on his own money. He never discusses it with me.'

'You've put something on the Captain yourself, I expect?' suggested Cribb.

'Yes, I got pretty fair odds on Monday from one of the bookies here.'

'Wise man,' said Cribb. 'Wish I'd had the foresight to do the same. Now tell me about Wednesday night, will you?'

'Wednesday?' Harvey looked vacant.

'The night Monk died. We're interested in your movements. Remember?'

'Oh. Wednesday. That was a grim enough evening, I can tell you. The Captain was as low in spirit as I've seen him. They'd given him a terrible buffeting on the outside track – he'd been forced to take his chances with them or retire from the race – and he was very short with me. But you've got to hand it to him. Come the time to get back on track there he was, ready to get among them again.'

'He was well ahead at that stage,' Cribb said in justification.

'Ah, yes. But I doubted whether he'd keep on his feet till Saturday. And he couldn't have thought so, either.'

'So you were out there watching him every step of the way?'

'I was, until one o'clock, when he came off.'

'Did you see anything of Sam Monk that night?' asked Cribb.

'I don't think I did.'

'And when Captain Chadwick came into the tent at one what shape was he in?'

Harvey shook his head sadly at the recollection.

'The poorest I've seen him. He could hardly move a muscle. He fell asleep while I was massaging him. I left him.'

'Where did you sleep? In the restaurant?'

'Yes. They haven't provided much for us attendants. I've spent every night in there so far.'

'See anyone else sleeping there?'

'I was generally too dead beat to notice.'

'All right,' said Cribb. 'Now, Mr Harvey. One thing you haven't explained. You spend all the week in constant attendance on your Captain. Then off you go today for a good four hours. What were you doing – trying to dodge me and my constables?'

Harvey smiled feebly.

'Not really. I was collecting this. I wouldn't stand a chance of getting one tomorrow. It was hard enough today.'

He was indicating the parcel he held in his lap.

'Let's have a look at it, then,' suggested Cribb.

Slowly and carefully the contents were revealed.

'What the devil!' exclaimed Thackeray.

'What is it then?' asked Cribb.

'Game pie,' answered Harvey. 'There's only one establishment in London that makes them like this, and the Captain will have no other. It's for his victory feast tomorrow night.'

'Hope it won't be wasted then,' commented Cribb. 'All

right, Mr Harvey. We'll keep you no longer. That's not to say I won't be seeing you again.'

When Harvey had left, Cribb added, 'Wouldn't count on him being in very good shape when I do, though.'

THE PEDESTRIAN CONTEST AT ISLINGTON

Positions at the end of the Fifth Day

Name	Miles	Laps
CAPT. ERSKINE CHADWICK	457	3
FEARGUS O'FLAHERTY	451	5
PETER CHALK	421	1
GEORGE WILLIAMS	420	4
FRANCIS MOSTYN-SMITH	419	3
JAMES GAFFNEY	408	0
DAVID STEVENS	405	1
MONTAGUE LAWTON	397	0
WILLIAM REID	363	4

16

Saturday

Thackeray could not be certain that the night was the coldest that week, but he knew positively that he had not passed such an uncomfortable four hours since he gave up beat pounding. There was a paraffin stove in the police office. His boot-welts were so near the flame that smoke rose from them. But his toes stayed bloodless all night. He had borrowed a spare great-coat and tried to insulate his already heavily clad body by tucking it around him as he settled in the one available armchair. It was no substitute for a heavy quilt over a decent horse-hair mattress. So he shivered and grumbled and shifted his bulky form about the creaking framework until five in the morning, when the duty constable put a mug of coffee in his hands. He sipped it dolefully.

Sergeant Cribb had left him in charge of the case.

'Things to check,' he had said cryptically. 'People to see. I may be out all of Saturday morning. You must be here through the night. Watch for anything irregular.

207

Now's the time people start getting jumpy. Be on the alert, Thackeray.'

Like the experienced constable he was, Thackeray interpreted this order to mean that he should be available and prepared to be roused from his sleep if anything happened. There was a duty constable in the Hall, and Thackeray ordered him in blunt terms to be faultlessly vigilant, and to wake him only for an extreme emergency or Sergeant Cribb's return. Cynically he suspected that Cribb's Saturday morning would be spent mainly in his own bed. Perhaps the Sergeant was justified in keeping his 'movements' to himself; he would need to be at his sharpest to trap the killer in the remaining time.

Thackeray finished his drink, and gripped the empty mug in his hands until he was sure it retained no more warmth. Then he stretched his limbs painfully, unwrapped the coat from around him, yawned and stood upright. A glance in a small mirror confirmed that his beard needed no trimming. He tightened his necktie and bent to lace his boots. Then he took up the dozen or so reports delivered to the office since Cribb's departure.

They were uniformly unhelpful. Where strychnine had been supplied the recipients were doctors whose names and addresses were provided and could be checked. The amounts were small, anyway. This line of inquiry had been totally without success. There were only hours remaining before the whole community that had pitched camp in the Hall broke up and scattered over the Metropolis. Nothing tangible had been found. They were still grappling with suspicions. And Cribb was at home sleeping.

208

Thackeray left the office and walked over to the track. There was plenty of activity there already. Herriott stood among his officials holding forth about the arrangements for this final day. A few reporters had arrived earlier than usual and were badgering the competitors, walking alongside them, demanding statements. There were even some genuine paying spectators, insomniacs probably, who stood or sat apart from each other, studiously isolated.

O'Flaherty was shuffling round at an impressive rate, untroubled now by sore feet. He was swinging his arms with apparent zest, and steadily overtaking rivals, still, it seemed, believing he could cut back Chadwick's lead.

You had to admire the Irishman's gameness, thought Thackeray. He was striving until the very finish. That bloated money-grabber, Herriott, was the only one who would benefit by O'Flaherty making a race of it. A close contest was a crowd-puller, all right. There would be a capacity crowd in by early evening, hoping for a super-human exhibition from O'Flaherty. Yet anyone who had followed the race day by day knew well enough that there could be only one result. Even if the Irishman drew level with Chadwick, the Champion would step up his pace and win. It was evident to any discriminating spectator that he was holding something in reserve. He had not needed Harvey's devious assistance.

Thackeray looked from man to man on the track, seeking out the stately gait of Erskine Chadwick. There was Reid, painfully limping, and Williams and Chalk, in conversation as usual; the two northerners were there, and the veteran who had shared Reid's hut; and Mostyn-Smith was just coming off for one of his rest periods. But Chadwick was not among them. No wonder O'Flaherty was going hell for leather!

It was even more worrying for Thackeray that no light was showing in Chadwick's tent. He hurried across to it and pulled back the flap, uncertain what to expect.

The tent was empty. The bed had been cleared and the blankets folded in military style. The air inside was cold. There was no sign that anyone had been there for hours.

Thackeray hurried to Herriott, who now stood alone.

'Have you seen Captain Chadwick, sir?'

'Chadwick? Yes, I saw him late last night, before he went out.'

'Out?' repeated Thackeray. 'Where to?'

'Didn't you hear? I thought you detectives knew everything that goes on here. He went off in a huff after Harvey failed to turn up to give him his massage last night.'

'When was this?'

'After one o'clock, when they all came off the track. There was no sign of Harvey, you see.'

'But he was here!' protested Thackeray. 'We interviewed him not two hours before.'

'I don't know anything about that,' said Herriott. 'All I know is that he wasn't about when Chadwick wanted him. The fellow came asking me if I'd seen Harvey. I told him I hadn't. I could see he was needled all right. Long time since I heard such words from one of the gentry.'

'Did he say where he was going?' asked Thackeray,

already dreading the prospect of explaining all this to his sergeant.

'Yes. He was planning to spend the night in the Turkish bath at Islington Green – only ten minutes away. They say it's a prime livener of the muscles.'

'And he hasn't been seen since?' said Thackeray, more to himself than Herriott. 'The race has been on an hour, and he hasn't shown up!'

'I shouldn't concern yourself,' Herriott advised. 'He'll be here any minute. He had a few miles in hand and he's in far better shape than O'Flaherty. I shouldn't wonder – why, there he is.'

There Chadwick unmistakably was, marching to his tent at the head of a gaggle of reporters. He wore an overcoat and muffler which he was removing even before he reached the tent. There was no sign of Harvey.

'Where's the trainer?' Thackeray asked Herriott.

The promoter shrugged his shoulders.

'No one's seen him since last night. Hooked it, I should think, after you grilled him. Your sergeant has a way of putting the fear of Old Nick into a man.'

Thackeray needed no reminding of this. His own palms were sweating at the thought of Cribb's return. Something had to be done. Harvey must be found.

He left Herriott and bore down rapidly on the police office, venting his fury on the duty constable.

'You let Chadwick leave the Hall last night, and failed to report it to me! He's been out all night, and only just got back. And Harvey, his trainer, has gone missing. I want him found, at once! Alert every bloody constable in the

211

building. Get everywhere searched. I'm going to question Chadwick.'

He confronted the Captain as he was making his way to the starting line. The exchange was necessarily short.

'I've got to find Mr Harvey, sir. Do you know his whereabouts?'

'No.'

'You haven't seen him since last night?'

'No. Out of my way, please.'

It was another hour before Harvey was found. The duty constable who brought the news to Thackeray was white-faced.

'He's in bad shape. They took him into a store-room by the main entrance and beat him about the head in there. When he fell they must have kicked his ribs for minutes on end.'

'He's too weak to talk, I suppose?' Thackeray asked without much sympathy in his tone.

'Hardly conscious at all. We're moving him to the infirmary as a matter of urgency. What bastards would have done this, do you think?'

'That's for you to find out,' Thackeray told him. 'My sergeant won't investigate, I can tell you. We've got our hands full enough. Harvey got what he asked for, anyway. You can't go round nobbling the opposition and expect to get away with it.'

'You think O'Flaherty's cronies did him over?'

'I'd start with them if there's no other clues,' suggested Thackeray. 'But there's other interests about – punters, bookies and their mob. I'd try to get Harvey to talk if

I was you. If he coughs anything useful to our inquiry you'll let me know at once, or I'll get you dismissed for incompetence.'

The news of the attack upon Harvey circulated quickly enough, but nobody except Chadwick seemed at all surprised or disturbed by the information. Rough tactics – boring and baulking, elbow-work and ankle-tapping – were accepted among these professionals, but Harvey's trick offended their code. It was furtive and cowardly. He was a snake in the grass, and when you catch a snake you don't toy with it.

Chadwick, deprived of his menial, had to adjust to new conditions – not easy in the final stages of a test of endurance. For the first time he appeared on the track unshaven. If he wanted water he would have to get it himself from the communal tap by the huts. At dawn he had coped without using any, but at midday, when he usually stopped for lunch, he would face the fifty yard walk if he wanted refreshment. The position of his tent, for so long an advantage, had become a handicap.

But Chadwick's visit to the Turkish bath had liberated his muscle-bound legs, and throughout the first two hours he was alternately running and walking, making up valuable yards on O'Flaherty, now reduced to a robot-like march. Although the Dublin Stag had won back nearly six miles during that first hour, and a close finish seemed in prospect, he looked a beaten man now.

The other sprightly performance on the track was Mostyn-Smith's. He had taken on a positively aggressive gait, with a pronounced forward tilt from the hips, and

213

arms working like piston-rods. His stride gained in speed rather than length, and he was still light of step. As he turned each time into the straight his spectacles flashed in a patch of light, demanding attention to his efforts. Behind them, no doubt, he was not seeing the amused spectators, but a newspaper advertisement for Dr Mostyn-Smith's Remedy for all Disorders, tested in the Six-Day Endurance Contest at the Agricultural Hall by its Maker.

Billy Reid was ambling towards the end of his stint with the caustic old ped who had shared his hut. The veteran had modified his approach.

'Take it nice and easy, young'un. No point in pushing it now. Save it up for the last hour or two. If you show you're nippy on your pins tonight you'll earn a shower of browns. They like a game fighter.'

Billy's lacerated feet were dictating his pace. To ease up would be as painful as to accelerate. He smiled in vague appreciation of the advice.

'There was a time – in the palmy days – when they'd have thrown sovereigns,' the old man reminisced. 'No chance of that tonight. They treat you according to pocket possibilities these days, and this ain't the well-greased contingent. Now at Brompton, fifteen years back, they lined up their carriages and pairs along the trackside. They was the gentry then, that watched us – princes and peers. Old Deerfoot got himself invited to the University to dine with the Prince of Wales, did you know that? A bloody Red Indian sitting down with royalty.'

'Don't bother me who watches,' said Reid, 'long as they let me finish in me own way.'

'They'll do that, lad. No one's going to stop a game boy—'

'They tried to stop the Irishman,' said Reid.

'O'Flaherty? Yes. The one that did that was paid out, though. Mind you play dumb when the bobbies come round. They'll find there's a lot of queer-sightedness among foot-racers. Nobody saw a bloody thing last night.'

It was a harassing morning for Thackeray. Rarely had he felt so ineffectual. Cribb shows confidence in him, gives him a responsible job, and what happens? Chadwick, a prime suspect, walks out of the Hall, out of police surveillance, for four hours, and nobody stops him. Harvey, another key man in the case, is savagely attacked in the building, and nobody knows who is responsible.

It might have helped if one of the many reports that arrived during the morning at the police office had brought news of the source of strychnine. That might have curbed Cribb's wrath. Thackeray hopefully examined every one; there was nothing of the least significance in any of them.

And there was another, worse setback to follow. Shortly after midday a constable arrived at the office with Sol Herriott in tow. The promoter was in a state of great agitation.

'You must do something,' he yelled at Thackeray. 'All the prize money – he's taken it all. Everything! A thousand pounds, near enough. My race is in ruins – hopeless. They've been running for six days and I can't pay them a penny. They'll kill me when they find out.'

'Someone's robbed you, you mean?' Thackeray struggled to assimilate this new information, scarcely believing his ill-luck.

'Jacobson – my friend for years! Opened the safe and took out all the prize money – bank-notes. He must have left the Hall this half-hour. I was talking to him—'

'Jacobson!'

The voice was angry. It was Cribb's. He was standing at the door. He addressed the young duty constable.

'You're in charge, then. See that nobody connected with the race leaves this hall for any reason. Understand?'

'Right, Sergeant.'

Cribb turned to Thackeray.

'Jacobson's the man we want. Mr Herriott, where's his lodgings?'

'Old Street. Over the "Three Ships",' answered the promoter, in a dazed voice.

'Come on,' said Cribb urgently. 'If he's only got half an hour on us we'll catch up with him there.'

17

Cribb was in earnest. For the first time since Thackeray had known him he was running – along the covered way leading from the Hall to Islington Green and Upper Street. And he was nimble on his feet. Although the oncoming crowds were too dense for his long legs to be of much use, the sergeant was adept at switching direction. Street vendors cluttered the corridor – match-sellers, sherbet-girls and piemen – surrounded by clusters of people. Cribb zig-zagged ahead until Thackeray lost sight of his nodding bowler. In Upper Street the sergeant had whistled a hansom, stated his destination and climbed in before Thackeray lumbered up. He held out a hand and hauled his breathless assistant aboard. The driver pulled his lever, the knee doors closed, and they were away.

The cabby had been promised double pay if he made good time. The vehicle lurched alarmingly as the horse was whipped towards Islington High Street. Inside, the two fares were jostled too much for a prolonged conversation.

'What if he ain't there?' Thackeray managed to get out.

'Too bad. We must take the chance,' Cribb answered. 'Reckon he'll make for a station after he's been home.'

There was no vehicle to compare with a hansom in slipping through streets thick with traffic. Soon they were rattling south along Goswell Road towards St Bart's, worming between growlers, buses, drays and barrows that loomed out of the patchy fog. The experience must have been unnerving even for the driver and he was in the safest position, perched high at the rear. Thackeray gripped the handrail until his knuckles whitened. He tried to focus on the horse's back rather than the obstacles hurtling towards them through the mist.

The hospital, a taller, darker mass, appeared ahead. The cab turned, its chassis groaning in protest, into Old Street.

'There's the pub!' shouted Cribb, above the racket of hooves and wheels. He looked up through the glass trap in the roof, but the cabby was already steering across the road towards 'The Three Ships.' How they escaped collision with a knifeboard bus being drawn at speed from the other direction, neither passenger knew.

'Wait here, for God's sake!' the sergeant called out as they jumped to the pavement and crossed to the entrance. Idlers around the door looked up in surprise at the urgent command. Somebody obviously needed his drink.

The public bar was doing a brisk trade for a Saturday. As Cribb weaved a route to the counter there were several half-formed threats, but something about his manner cut them short. Thackeray remained at the door; Cribb's figure was better suited to side-on progress than his.

'One moment, landlord.'

Cribb's voice was more insistent than any of the pleas around him for refills.

'Sir.'

'Police business. You've a man living over these premises, I believe.'

The licensee was a pale, rabbit-like man. He almost dropped a full glass at hearing Cribb's announcement.

'That's right, guv'nor. Mr Jacobson. I haven't seen 'im for a day or two.'

'Not at all today?'

'No guv. But I'm busy, as you can see. He may be up there now, for all I know. The door's round the back. Up the iron staircase.'

Cribb forced a passage towards the back exit and found the stairs. He was up them three at a time, and knocked hard at the frosted window, trying to peer through. There was no reply. Instinct told him Jacobson was not inside hiding. He clattered down, ran across the yard and round to the front of the building, surprising Thackeray by opening the bar door and hauling him outside.

'Not there.' Cribb was at a loss.

Putting his unhappy morning out of mind, Thackeray acted with inspiration. Twenty yards up the street, at the entrance to another bar, was a barrel organist, playing a genuine shoulder-instrument supported on a pole. The constable barked in his ear, above the wheezing intake of air and 'Champagne Charlie.'

'D'you see a man call a cab out here this last half-hour? Probably carried a case.'

'Eh?' The musician inclined his head to Thackeray, continuing to turn his grinding-handle.

Thackeray repeated the question, and produced a coin from his pocket. It was an instant aid to the man's hearing.

'Quarter of an hour back I saw the gent from upstairs come down with a case. Couldn't get no 'ansom. Took a four-wheeler, 'e did.'

'Did you hear where he was making for?' bellowed the constable, slipping the hand into his pocket again.

'Matter o' fact I did.' The organist waited until the second coin was in his hand. 'The station, 'e said. Fenchurch Street. Reckon 'e was going east.'

They turned to their cab. The driver was by the horse, chatting with a passer-by and swinging his arms for warmth.

'Right driver!' Cribb called imperatively. 'Fenchurch Street – and get this beast at the gallop!'

They clambered aboard. The whip cracked above their heads and the pursuit began anew. A right turn into City Road and a long, hard chase towards Moorgate. By the Artillery Barracks they had to swerve to miss a cat's-meat barrow parked at the roadside. The road was badly pot-holed. If the horse had stumbled anywhere the detectives would have been pitched straight out of the front. But the cabby kept up the reckless canter, even encouraging the animal with bloodcurdling bellows. Police, the passengers had said they were. They should have their gallop.

The City was quiet, or he would never have taken them down past the Bank and up Lombard Street. But the fog was thicker here and in the narrower street he had to rein and come into line behind a coal cart. Its rate was agonizingly slow. At Lime Street he turned left and cantered between the tall buildings, taking a chance on the narrow passage being clear. Along Fenchurch Avenue, into Billiter Street, and they were back in Fenchurch Street, ahead of the cart. A wave of the whip, a shrieking turn, and they were in the station approach, rattling across cobbles.

'We'll be back!' Cribb shouted. He sprinted into the booking-hall, darted his eyes across the scene, and made for the stairs. Thackeray was not far behind.

The main area of the station was almost deserted, but it was two or three minutes before they discovered this, for the fog had cut visibility to twenty yards or so.

There was only one train waiting, and that was not attracting many passengers.

'Where's this one bound for?' Cribb asked a porter, neat in monkey jacket and corduroys.

Weighing up the sergeant as second-class, no more, the porter jerked his thumb at the board behind him and moved away.

'Tilbury. Come on, Thackeray.'

They bustled past an indignant ticket collector with a peremptory 'Police.' Then they began checking the carriages, small, four-door affairs with oil lamps alight inside them. It was not a long train, and in three minutes they were by the hissing tank engine.

'Got away, Sarge,' Thackeray sighed, producing a handkerchief to mop his forehead.

'When did the last train leave?' Cribb shouted to the driver and fireman, who leaned in some interest from their cab.

221

'From this platform, you mean—' began the driver. 'Hey! Git off that bloody line!'

But Thackeray was away. He had glimpsed a fast-moving figure on the opposite platform and taken the straighter route in that direction. He clambered up the other side and set off in pursuit. His speed was a revelation.

Cribb too bolted along his platform, wishing he had a police-rattle to sound the hue and cry. Thackeray was out ahead on the other side of the train, but Cribb could not see whether he was gaining on the runaway figure. He reached the ticket barrier and brushed past the irate official in time to see the constable still running hard. An instant later the fog swallowed him.

Cribb made for the same direction. Ahead, he heard the constable thudding down the stairs towards the booking-hall. Then a shout and the sound of someone falling. A scuffle ahead, and two figures wrestling at the foot of the stairs.

'Lay off him, Thackeray,' Cribb ordered, when he was near enough to assist.

'All right – I'll give no trouble.' The voice was Jacobson's. 'The money's all here in the case.'

'Must have lain low as we walked past his carriage, Sarge. I saw him getting up on the other platform,' explained Thackeray with some pride.

'As pretty a piece of arresting as I've seen. Fine work, Thackeray. Now, Mr Jacobson. We'll get you back to the Hall, I think. I'd like to see who's winning that race.'

Cribb did not get back to Islington as early as he planned. Jacobson's arrest made certain formalities necessary. The prisoner was taken to a police station and charged with theft. And after a long wrangle it was conceded by the local force that Cribb should take custody of Jacobson. Then the detectives sat down to their first meal since breakfast. By seven o'clock that evening they were ready to return.

The drive to the Hall with Jacobson was reassuringly sedate. Cribb hired a 'growler' and ordered the driver to take his time – a superfluous instruction as things turned out. In the City even the street-lamps were obscured by the fog. Drivers of hansoms were compelled to walk leading their horses. Nothing could move at a faster rate than they dictated.

The delays greatly disturbed Thackeray. More than once he got down from the four-wheeler and strutted along the line of traffic in front, looking for a cause of the hold-up.

'We'll be deuced lucky to make the Hall by ten, at this rate,' he complained as he climbed aboard again.

Cribb was disturbingly serene. His usual sense of urgency was absent and this made Thackeray uneasy. The constable had relished Jacobson's capture as a taste of action after days of patient questioning. But had it helped the main inquiry? Wasn't it just a diversion, like Harvey's sabotage of O'Flaherty, that the local force should have dealt with?

Jacobson sat in silence, staring through Cribb. He did not want to talk, and the sergeant made no approach. But his presence was inhibiting. If he was a vital witness, or the killer – and why else should they take custody of him? – it would be disastrous to discuss the case. So Thackeray persisted in his agitated excursions while the others waged silence on each other.

The carriage reached Islington High Street a few minutes after nine o'clock. The isolating barrier of fog had muffled all sound, but now there was shouting immediately outside. The carriage halted on the fringe of an ugly, jostling mob. Cribb opened the door with difficulty, settled the fare, and, taking a tight grip on Jacobson's upper arm, guided him towards the Hall entrance. But it was there that the crowd was converging. They were people who had been refused admittance. Every seat, every standing place, a harassed official was trying to explain, was taken. Nobody else would be allowed in.

This was a challenge almost designed for Thackeray. He put thumb and forefinger between his teeth and produced a whistle worthy of the Regent's Park parrot house. A police helmet could be glimpsed at the entrance, and Thackeray exchanged a signal with its wearer. Then, to surprisingly few protests, a passage was cleared from both sides of the crowd. Cribb, with his prisoner, and Thackeray with the prize money slipped through and into the Hall.

'Get this man to the police office and see he's kept there,' Cribb ordered Thackeray at once. 'And be discreet,' he added, touching a finger to his lips. 'I'll return the money.'

'Who shall we see after that, Sarge?' Thackeray asked. 'There's precious little time left.'

'Don't propose seeing anyone,' Cribb told him, with a glance that infuriated him, it was so expressionless. 'Not till after the race is over, any rate. There's time to enjoy it, Thackeray. Chance to take a look at some pucka foot-racers – not station platform performers.'

The nine surviving competitors were certainly giving a lively performance. True to theatrical tradition they had reserved something for the last night. Three, Chadwick, Chalk and Mostyn-Smith, had decked themselves in new running-costumes, stored at the bottom of their portman-teaux with this evening in mind. Chadwick and Chalk wore blue; the Captain's silk drawers were in his univer-sity colour, and the Scythebearer had put on a favourite jersey hooped in white and indigo. But Mostyn-Smith had undeniably scooped the fashion parade with a bright vermilion jersey and minimal orange knickerbockers over white tights.

There was no carnival costume for O'Flaherty. He had used the day grimly reducing the lead, yard by yard. With just over an hour left he was only a mile in arrears, but it was clear to experienced observers that the chase was futile. Chadwick had decided to pace himself through the last few hours in order to win; he was not interested in the distance he achieved. So he was performing at calculated intervals, running strongly for five or six laps and then stepping off the track to talk with friends or stand with hand on hips watching the others. He was in control of the race, and he intended it to be known.

Not many of the crowd appreciated the true position, and the cheering mounted hour by hour as the scoreboard gave its information. The underdog was giving chase, and gaining steadily. On the stands boots thundered in unison until the building seemed to vibrate. The usual chanting and catcalling was lost in breakers of cheering that rolled and boomed and crashed towards the track. At one end, the bandsmen might have been acting a mime for all but a small section of the crowd around them.

In the centre was Sol Herriott. He, too, had dressed to impress, in silk topper, white tie, white waistcoat and tails, the uniform of a music hall manager. He smiled expansively and continuously, his composure restored by Cribb's recovery of the prize money. He was supervising, in a perfunctory way, the erection of a presentation stand. It was a pity he could not now delegate the task to Jacobson, but he enjoyed being in the centre, and the workmen seemed capable enough.

There was not much talking done on the track. The competitors were absorbed in their task, and anyway it was necessary to shout to be heard. Chalk did run alongside Williams for a few paces. The Half-breed was interested in the work going on in the centre.

'What in 'ell's that lot for?' he bellowed to Chalk.

'Can't you see, mate? That's the bloody scaffold. When this lot's over they're going to pick on the weakest man and string 'im up for killing Darrell. Keep some wind in store, mate. You might need it when the Law comes for you.'

The race entered its last half-hour. Chadwick waited for O'Flaherty to trudge past the point where he was standing, and then joined him, easily matching his stride. Mostyn-Smith, apparently revitalized by his startling appearance, slipped past them both like a thoroughbred passing cabhorses. No one else came up to his form, but it could at least be said that every competitor was moving with a sense of purpose. Even young Reid had summoned a grotesque trotting action for these final minutes.

Chadwick remained at O'Flaherty's shoulder, moving smoothly, with the clear promise of power in hand. When perhaps a quarter of an hour was left, the Irishman's supporters (the majority present) realized his chance of victory was past. The cheering diminished and was replaced by sympathetic applause and generous suggestions for downing Chadwick. The race was an exhibition now, and the crowd responded as they would at a prize-fight, tossing coins in appreciation. Several of the performers unashamedly stooped to pick up and pocket silver pieces. But the rain was mostly of the copper sort, and some, released from vantage points in the vaulting, struck its recipients painfully.

A bell was rung to mark the start of the final minute. Chadwick shot away from O'Flaherty, accelerating astonishingly, stretching his stride and bracing himself to a 'style.' He had misjudged the mood of the audience. Fruit hurtled about his head until he stopped his display – a rejected peacock.

Reinforcements of police were now around the track and in the bookmakers' enclosure. Officials, too, surrounded the circuit, ready with numbered flags to mark the finishing points.

A gun fired. The nine survivors halted with almost military precision.

227

Chadwick's arms were raised in triumph. A tomato thudded and split on his varsity jersey. The band declared their presence with 'The Conquering Hero'. Herriott shouted through a megaphone that a presentation would take place in fifteen minutes. Thousands streamed through the exits.

'They're all going, Sarge!' Thackeray announced in alarm to Cribb. They stood watching Chadwick walk easily to his tent. The other athletes, and some of the crowd, grovelled on the track for pennies and farthings.

'That's right. It's over.'

'But the charge! We ain't charged anyone yet.'

'Time for that. Let's see the prize-giving.' The crowd was down to a few hundred when Herriott mounted the rostrum, clutching the precious case with the prize money. He made a short speech, mainly self-laudatory, reviewing the race. Then Chadwick, freshly changed into a suit, accepted his award. He was followed by O'Flaherty, who was helped on and off the platform. The third place went to Mostyn-Smith – good enough to claim on every box and bottle that he sold for the next thirty years. There were small awards for the other finishers – even Billy Reid, the last man, whose brother came forward in his place to receive the money.

Herriott addressed the Press.

'Well, gentlemen, I must thank you for your support during these six long days. The race has not been uneventful, I am sure you will agree. Perhaps you, like my loyal officials, will be grateful for the chance of a night's slumber. I know that I shall. But I venture to think that when we have all recovered our lost sleep we may look back on this enterprise as a notable sporting occasion.'

There was a ripple of unenthusiastic clapping. Herriott descended to ground level. Cribb was waiting for him. He spoke confidentially.

'Can't let you have that sleep just yet, Mr Herriott. Got to clear up the Darrell business. I'd be obliged if we could talk in your office, sir. We'll go casual-like, and the newsmen won't catch on.'

THE PEDESTRIAN CONTEST AT ISLINGTON

Final Positions

		Miles	
1.	CAPTAIN ERSKINE CHADWICK	538	Wins £500 and the Belt
2.	FEARGUS O'FLAHERTY	537	Receives £100
3.	FRANCIS MOSTYN-SMITH	512	Receives £50
4.	PETER CHALK	495	Receives £10
5.	GEORGE WILLIAMS	494	Receives £10
6.	JAMES GAFFNEY	467	Receives £10
7.	DAVID STEVENS	460	Receives £10
8.	MONTAGUE LAWTON	454	Receives £5
9.	WILLIAM REID	409	Receives £5
10.	MATTHEW JENKINS	200	
11.	WALTER HOLLAND	192	
12.	CHARLES JONES	188	
13.	GEORGE STOCKWELL	139	
14.	CHARLES DARRELL (deceased)	126	
15.	PETER LUCAS	78	
16.	JOSEPH MARTINDALE	61	

18

Sol Herriott toyed with a large, unlit cigar, rolling it gently between his palms. The detectives had refused cigars. A pity, that. After the success of the race he was feeling expansive.

'How about a drink, gentlemen? Not on duty now, eh?'

Thackeray looked to Cribb for a lead. They were seated in armchairs to the side of Herriott's desk.

'Hardly, sir,' the sergeant answered. 'But there are points to clear up, you know, so we'll leave the drinks for later, if you don't mind.'

'Of course.' He produced matches, and lit the cigar. The smoke obscured his vision, and he waved it away. 'Points, you say. What do you mean, Sergeant?'

'Well, there's the matter of the dog.'

Cribb paused for effect. Thackeray, quite mystified, did not flinch. Herriott looked up in surprise.

'The dog?'

'Yes sir. Sam Monk's dog.'

Again he stopped, and by his expression expected Herriott to respond.

Herriott cleared his throat. He was uncomfortable under Cribb's scrutiny.

'Well, Sergeant. What is this about Monk's dog?'

'Lovely animal, sir.'

'Er – so I believe,' he chanced.

'If no one cares for it, we'll have to put it down. Costs a shilling or two to feed, you see.'

Apprehension shifted like a cloud-shadow from Herriott's face.

'Oh, indeed. That's it, is it? I'm sure we can find a home for the beast. Leave that with me, Sergeant.' He stood up. 'I think I'll have a drink, anyway. You won't join me?'

Thackeray shook his head. Cribb was silent. Seconds passed, and Herriott's confidence began to drain again. He gulped some gin. At length, he spoke again.

'There is something else, Sergeant?'

'Oh yes,' Cribb replied, as though he had needed reminding. 'Jacobson. You know, he's told us a queer story. Would you like to tell us yours, sir?'

'You've already had mine, Sergeant.'

'That's right, sir. There's nothing just come to mind that you previously forgot?'

Herriott paled. In seconds, he was sure, Cribb would drop the cloak of courtesy. And questions would follow in dagger-thrusts. He precipitated the crisis.

'That's a damned insulting remark, Sergeant! I'm a man of honour, and I most strongly resent your insinuations. You can keep your Scotland Yard methods for the vulgar mob outside. They won't do for me! I'll soon inform your superior.' He stubbed out the cigar and stood

232

up. 'As I've nothing else to tell you, I think you'd better leave now.'

Cribb remained in his chair.

'If we do, Mr Herriott, I'll thank you to accompany me to the Islington Police Station.'

Herriott sank down again, sighing resignedly. 'Very well. What do you want to know from me?'

'The blackmail,' answered Cribb. He stopped to study Herriott.

'Blackmail?'

There was a long silence. Herriott looked desperately towards his visitors, his eyes pleading them to speak. They did not. Finally, he took a long draught of gin and began to talk.

'You've been listening to Jacobson's lies. He's not a balanced man, Sergeant. I've done what I can to help him, as you know, but—' He spread his hands in a gesture of helplessness. 'He showed no gratitude. On the contrary, he seemed to dislike me. Possibly it was the strain of responsibility. We certainly had our setbacks during the last few days. In some way, he seemed to hold me responsible. Said his nerves couldn't take any more and he wanted to quit. I told him, quite justly, he'd have to honour his contract, or he couldn't be paid. He became abusive.'

Herriott was encouraged by Cribb's silent attention.

'When I refused to pay him, he began to threaten me. Perhaps you got him to admit this?'

He looked hopefully at Cribb, but there was no response. After mopping his forehead with a handkerchief, Herriott continued.

'He tried to make me believe that you had to make an arrest for the murders, and you'd grab the first man you could. He talked about the bad reputation of the old Detective Branch, and the corruption that came to light in the Home Office inquiry. Of course, I dismissed such specious rubbish. I've always found the police entirely honourable.'

He flashed an ingratiating smile at the detectives.

'And then,' he went on, 'Jacobson made me understand what he was threatening. He knew I'd been out on the evening before Darrell died. He said he would fabricate a story that I had been dining with Mrs Darrell. He demanded money from me, made me open the safe. So I was forced to pay him. I don't need to tell you what happened after that, do I?'

He groped for the gin bottle and refilled his glass.

At last Cribb broke his silence.

'You say you respect the police. Why pay up?'

'Lost my head,' admitted Herriott. 'Panicked.'

'You know Mrs Darrell socially. What's so incriminating about a dinner out with her? I've heard her talk of you as an old friend.'

'People misconstrue things, Sergeant.'

'Then it's up to you to speak the truth, ain't it?' snapped Cribb, animated at last. 'Look, I know that you *were* with Cora Darrell that evening. You told me you dined alone at the London Sporting Club. I checked there this morning, and they hadn't seen you for a fortnight. Then I got the truth from Cora Darrell. You're full of lies, aren't you? You told us Jacobson had robbed you, when you'd just paid

234

him off to silence him. You had your reasons for keeping quiet about that dinner date with Cora, didn't you?'

Herriott had disintegrated as rapidly as his story. He was deathly pale, and trembling.

Cribb pounced.

'What made you sign the poison register in an assumed name?'

For a moment the question stunned Herriott. Cribb produced a sheaf of papers from his inner pocket an tossed them on to the desk.

'These are all reports on sales of strychnine—'

Herriott snatched one up.

'No! By God! You can't have found ...' He checked himself. 'Which poison register? What do you mean?'

Cribb was completely in control.

'If you want me to produce the dispenser who served you ...'

Even Thackeray's eyebrows jumped at this. For Herriott it meant capitulation. He sunk his face into his hands.

'It's all over!' he mumbled. 'All over. Why couldn't you have stayed out of this? It's only because of you Monk had to go. If you had kept your nose out of it I'd never have had to finish him. He's on my conscience, and he should be on yours, too. Bloody Darrell got what he deserved. Monk was different.'

Thackeray was writing furiously in his notebook.

'Never mind Monk,' snapped Cribb. 'Why did you poison Darrell? You did that for Cora, didn't you?'

Herriott acknowledged this with a slight gesture of his hand, and then covered his eyes again.

235

Cribb continued.

'You met her in the weeks before the race, while you were watching Darrell's breathings at Hackney. And when she flashed her pretty eyes your way, you saw an invitation in them, didn't you? But being the man you are, you held back. You're no philanderer, Mr Herriott, whatever else you might be.'

Herriott's bowed head registered nothing.

'I dare say she told you her story during those weeks,' Cribb went on, '– a snatch here and there as she made some excuse to exchange a few words with you. And you swallowed it all – misunderstood wife, bullying brute of a husband.'

The twitch of Herriott's shoulders confirmed Cribb's account.

'But Cora miscalculated. She got your sympathy. Got dined out on it while her husband was foot-slogging last Monday night. But she didn't know you were planning on marriage once her brute of a husband was neatly boxed up and six feet under. She didn't know you were the scrupulous sort, Mr Herriott – a man that wouldn't take another man's wife while that man was still alive. She couldn't have known you'd already bought the strychnine.'

Herriott looked up.

'That's right. She had no part in the plan. She knew nothing.' He laughed grimly. 'She knew as little of me as I know of her. It took Jacobson to tell me what sort of creature she really is – too late, of course. It seems she gives herself to anyone she fancies when her husband is racing.'

'But you really believed she wanted to marry you?'

Herriott nodded.

'I was completely taken in. Believe me, last Monday evening was the first time we'd ever dined alone. But I'd already planned to release her from this misery that she described. I wasn't going to say anything to her, though.' He sighed. 'It all went wrong, of course. I doctored Darrell's tonic that night. I'd sent Jacobson away to get a change of clothes, after he'd ruined his suit in the fire. Monk was out of the Hall. I slipped into Darrell's tent and tipped the poison into the bottle. I thought Darrell wouldn't touch it until he was exhausted, in the last days of the race. Instead he took it that second morning. He was dead in no time at all.'

Cribb nodded and took up the narrative.

'We didn't put it down to tetanus or heart failure, so your plan went wrong. You had to provide us with a culprit. Monk was the obvious choice. But how did you force him to write the note?'

'There was no force in it, Sergeant. It was pure luck. He was an illiterate man, you know. When he thought that tetanus was the cause of death he felt responsible. He shouldn't have let Darrell run barefoot, you see. So he asked me to help him write a note to Cora. Afterwards, I saw that it made a perfect suicide note.'

'And you fixed him at night, after Jacobson had left him in the hut?'

'Yes. I could walk about the tents and huts as a matter of routine. But even that went wrong. I shouldn't have stunned him. You would never have known. But you did find out – and the rest is a nightmare.'

'Jacobson, you mean?'

'That bloody idiot! Yes. He unknowingly stumbled on the one thing that could incriminate me – my evening with Cora Darrell. I was ready to pay anything to keep you from investigating that relationship. So I opened the safe, and he took what he wanted.'

'What made you report it as a theft?'

'What else could I do? The runners had to be paid tonight. If there was no money they'd have been on me like starving hounds. I gave Jacobson a reasonable time to escape, and then informed you. I couldn't announce at the last minute that the money had been taken. That's been tried before, and you know what happens. I don't believe they'd have left one brick of this Hall standing, and God knows what they'd have done to me. I hoped that if the word got round in time, the story of theft might be believed. Jacobson might have got clean away, and I could have paid off the debts later. As you know, it didn't happen like that.' Herriott slumped, exhausted, over the desk.

'Come on, Thackeray,' said Cribb. 'We'll get him down to the local station. He needs a rest – even if it is in a cell. What's the time? Before midnight is it? Just made it in the six days.'

'I'd like to know how you got Jacobson to talk,' said Thackeray. He and Cribb were being transported out of Islington by hansom.

'Jacobson? Never said a word.'

Thackeray was incredulous.

238

'Well, if he didn't, whatever led you to Herriott, Sarge?'

'Process of elimination,' Cribb declared. 'Why should anyone kill a man like Darrell – good runner, popular celebrity?'

'For profit, I thought,' admitted Thackeray.

'That was the first possibility. Someone with a lot to win on the race. But look at the suspects. Chadwick? He expected to win. Didn't need to kill the opposition.'

'That's true, Sarge. But Darrell went ahead, and surprised him proper. Chadwick could have decided to poison him after that.'

'Not so,' said Cribb. 'He wouldn't have had the strychnine ready. Couldn't have walked into Darrell's tent, come to that. Now Harvey—'

'*He* was a worried man,' said Thackeray. 'He would have killed, I'm sure.'

'Might have,' agreed Cribb. 'He wanted watching. Could have had some strychnine with him too, as a tonic for Chadwick.'

'What made you discount him, then?'

'The second murder. Monk's note. Man like him couldn't get Monk to write his own suicide note. Harvey didn't get on with Monk.'

'All right. It couldn't have been Harvey. What about Jacobson? He was a man in plenty of financial trouble.'

'Couldn't get a bet on, though. Every bookie in London knew he was in debt. No profit for him in killing Darrell. That's why he had to blackmail Herriott.'

Thackeray was convinced.

'You don't need to go through the other suspects,

Sarge. You was left with Herriott and Cora Darrell. Cora wanted to keep her husband.'

'Good. You realized that,' Cribb congratulated him. 'Her story rattled like this old hansom. In all the lies she told – and there were plenty – one fact shone through. Her fury at Darrell's death, whatever the cause. He was just coming into the big money. Star billing. She didn't want him killed.'

'Why did she cover up so much, then, Sarge?'

'Understandable,' said Cribb. 'Lonely wife takes a lover or two. Don't look so good when husband gets murdered, does it? Scandal, Thackeray. Powerful force. Could ruin a woman's chance of remarrying. People have lively imaginations where philanderings are concerned. So I was left with Herriott, and then it had to be a crime of passion, you see. Profit couldn't be the motive. We found out from the maid that Cora dined out that Monday with someone. Cora tried to cover up with a false story, so it had to be someone we would know. That had to be Herriott – the only man out of the Hall that evening. It was – I confirmed that by checking on their stories. But it still wasn't proof of murder. I needed a confession.'

'But you had the report in from the place where he bought the strychnine,' Thackeray pointed out. 'That was evidence enough.'

'Pure bluff,' said Cribb. 'Still got no idea where the stuff came from. It broke him, though, didn't it?'

The cab turned into the street where Thackeray lived. Before climbing out, the constable addressed a final question to Cribb.

'If you knew it was him, Sarge, why didn't you confront him earlier? We might all have got home before now.'

'That would have ended the race too soon. Done the peds out of their money.'

'You did it for them?'

'Not really. Ain't a betting man myself. Never have been. But Mrs Cribb had ten quid on Chadwick. Goodnight to you.'

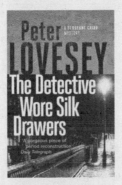

Forbidden in Victorian England, the grim and violent world
of bare-knuckle fighting has gone underground. So when
a headless body is found floating in the Thames, his hands
'pickled' for fighting, Sergeant Cribb knows he
is facing a challenge.

Desperate for information, they select the young constable
Henry Jago to infiltrate the gang, subjecting him to a
rigorous programme of purging, pickling and training.
Cribb is certain that the losing fighters are being killed, or
worse, so getting Jago out just in time is crucial ...

*

'A rich and unusual mystery, with suspense enough for the
most confirmed addict'
Los Angeles Times

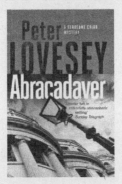

A practical joker is haunting the popular music halls of
Victorian London – but far from being funny, his intentions
are deeply sinister. A trapeze artist misses her timing
when the ropes are shortened; a comedian who invites the
audience to sing along with him finds the words of his song
'shamefully' altered; mustard has been applied to a sword
swallower's blade; a singer's costume has been rigged;
the girl in a magician's box is trapped.

And then the mischief escalates to murder. Or was murder
intended all along? The indomitable detective team of
Sergeant Cribb and Constable Thackeray dive into the back
rooms and dark alleyways of London as they
pursue the elusive criminal..

*

'Sinister fun in splendidly atmospheric setting'
Sunday Telegraph